**"You're important** Gina.

"My family and I need you here, Zach. You're not going to quit, are you?"

"I wouldn't do that. But you should know that I intend to honor my promise to Lucky. I'll do what I can to change your mind."

"Try away. It won't work."

With her chin up and the confident smile on her mouth, she was irresistible.

"That sounds like a challenge—and I like challenges," he said, advancing toward her. "Did you mean that?"

"I... Did I mean what?"

"About me trying to convince you." Her eyes were the prettiest color, green with little flecks of brown and gold. "Did you?"

He brushed the silky lock back from her face and tucked it behind her ear. Her pupils dilated and he knew she felt some of what he did. She touched her lips with the tip of her tongue in what he recognized as a nervous gesture.

"I—"

He laid his finger over her soft lips. "Shh." Tipping up her chin, he leaned down.

Dear Reader,

This is the fifth (and last) book set in Saddlers Prairie, a fictitious ranching town in Montana prairie country. But don't worry—I'll be back soon with new love stories set in a new fictitious town.

Gina Arnett grew up in Saddlers Prairie and left as soon as she graduated from high school. Now she's back, but not by choice. Her uncle Lucky has left her his ailing ranch, a ranch Gina doesn't want.

Foreman Zach Horton is a man with a past he keeps buried—and a mission. He promised Gina's uncle that he would stick around long enough to convince her to keep the ranch.

Neither of them expects to find love, especially with each other. I hope you enjoy their story.

Happy reading!

Ann Roth

I always appreciate hearing from readers. Email me at ann@annroth.net, or write me at P.O. Box 25003, Seattle, WA 98165-1903, or visit my Facebook page. And please visit my website at www.annroth.net, where you can enter the monthly drawing to win a free book! Be sure to visit the Fun Stuff page, where you'll find my blog and all sorts of fun stuff.

# A RANCHER'S CHRISTMAS

—

## ANN ROTH

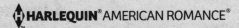
HARLEQUIN® AMERICAN ROMANCE®

To cowboys everywhere and the people who love them.

Recycling programs
for this product may
not exist in your area.

ISBN-13: 978-0-373-75476-2

A RANCHER'S CHRISTMAS

Copyright © 2013 by Ann Schuessler

Printed in U.S.A.

## ABOUT THE AUTHOR

Ann Roth lives in the greater Seattle area with her husband. After earning an MBA she worked as a banker and corporate trainer. She gave up the corporate life to write, and if they awarded PhDs in writing happily-ever-after stories, she'd surely have one.

Ann loves to hear from readers. You can write her at P.O. Box 25003, Seattle, WA 98165-1903 or email her at ann@annroth.net.

### Books by Ann Roth

**HARLEQUIN AMERICAN ROMANCE**

*Saddlers Prairie

# BREAKFAST CASSEROLE

*18 eggs*

*2 tbsp milk*

*1 tsp parsley*

*½ tsp dill weed*

*¼ tsp pepper*

*1 can undiluted mushroom soup*

*3 tbsp sherry*

*4 tbsp butter*

*¼ pound sliced mushrooms*

*¼ cup chopped onion*

*6 strips bacon, cooked and crumbled*

*1½ cup each, shredded and mixed together:*

*jack cheese and sharp cheddar*

*Paprika*

Grease a 9" x 11" casserole dish.

Beat eggs with milk, parsley, dill weed and pepper, and set aside. In a saucepan, stir soup and sherry until hot and smooth. Remove from heat and let cool slightly.

Melt the butter in a pan. Add mushrooms and onion and sauté 5 minutes. Add egg mixture and crumbled bacon to the pan and cook until the eggs are softly set. Remove from heat. Spoon half the egg mixture into the casserole. Cover with half the soup mixture, then half the cheese. Repeat. Sprinkle the top layer with paprika. May be refrigerated overnight.

Preheat the oven to 350°F. Bake uncovered until hot and bubbly, about 30–35 minutes if unrefrigerated or for an hour if refrigerated.

Let stand 10 minutes, then cut into squares.

# Chapter One

Gina was rushing out to get herself another espresso before the upcoming meeting when her office phone rang. Knowing that it might be someone from Grant Industries, she lunged toward her desk before her assistant, Carrie, picked up. "This is Gina Arnett."

"It's Uncle Redd."

Of all times for him to call.

"Hi," she said. "I know I haven't phoned you lately, but I've been in a real crunch here, working on that holiday promotion for Grant Industries—the big retailer I told you about last time we talked. If they like the results from the campaign I've put together, they'll put me on retainer for them for the next year."

Plus she'd earn a fat year-end bonus, which she really, really needed.

She checked her watch. Still time to race down to the coffee bar and get that espresso—if she hurried. "We're rolling out part two of our Holiday Magic campaign tomorrow, and you wouldn't believe how busy I am right now. Can I call you back tonight?"

"I need to tell you something, Gina," her uncle said in a solemn tone Gina had rarely heard. "I'm afraid it can't wait."

She frowned. "What's happened?"

Uncle Redd usually cut straight to the chase, and this time was no different. "Sometime during the night, your uncle Lucky had a heart attack. He's gone."

"Gone?" She sank onto her desk chair.

"I'm afraid so." Her uncle cleared his throat. "How soon can you get home?"

It had been almost seven years since she'd visited there. The last time had been for her mother's funeral. She remembered the long flight from Chicago to Billings and the shorter connecting flight to Miles City, followed by a forty-mile drive to Saddlers Prairie. Getting there would take the better part of a day.

"I'll need to check with the airlines and get back to you," she said. "When do you need me there?"

"As soon as possible. Seeing as how Thanksgiving is next week, we decided to hold the funeral right away. We scheduled it for this coming Friday—three days from now."

Funeral.

The news finally sank in. Uncle Lucky was dead. Their little family just kept shrinking. Gina's shoulders sagged.

"Do you need help with airfare?" her uncle asked.

"No, Uncle Redd. I'm thirty years old and I make a good living." Never mind that most of her credit cards were just about maxed out. Nobody needed to know that. "As soon as I book the flight, I'll call with my arrival information. Or would you rather I rented a car?"

"Waste your money like that? There's no need, honey. I'll be waiting for you at the baggage claim."

Uncle Redd made a choking sound, and Gina suspected he was crying. Uncle Lucky had been his last living brother and they'd been close.

Gina had also been close to him, had spent most every

summer of her childhood at his Lucky A ranch. She teared up, too.

Lately, Uncle Lucky had been begging her to come back and visit, saying he missed her and needed to talk to her about something important. Now she'd never know what he'd wanted to say.

Why hadn't she made more of an effort?

She managed to tell her uncle goodbye before she hung up. She was sniffling and looking up the number for the airline on her smartphone when the com line buzzed.

"It's me," her assistant whispered. "Where are you? Everyone's here."

By everyone, she meant Evelyn Grant, the great-granddaughter of William Grant and Grant Industries' first female CEO. That she'd even come to the meeting showed how important this campaign was to her. She wouldn't like to be kept waiting.

There was no time to grieve. Gina wiped her eyes, grabbed her iPad and left for the meeting room.

LATER THAT AFTERNOON, Gina sat in her office with Carrie reviewing what needed to be done with each of their clients when Gina's boss, Kevin, knocked on the door. Wearing an elegant cashmere coat and scarf over his bespoke suit, he looked put-together, handsome and successful. Sure, he was a bit on the ruthless side and on his third marriage, but careerwise, Kevin was her kind of man.

Someday, Gina hoped to meet and fall in love with someone with her boss's drive and determination. "Carrie and I are just reviewing my client to-do list," she said. "What can I do for you, Kevin?"

"Are you sure you can handle the Grant campaign from Montana?"

This was the third time he'd asked her that question

since she'd told him about her uncle's passing. "Absolutely," she repeated with a reassuring smile.

As the only member of her family under seventy, she would be expected to handle her uncle's estate, meet with the attorney and cull his papers and personal effects before Uncle Redd moved into the house and took over the ranch.

But that shouldn't consume too much of her time, and she was sure she would still have plenty of opportunities to focus on her job. "Anything I can't do from there, Carrie will take care of. She's been in on this campaign from the start and she's up to speed on everything. And don't forget that next week is Thanksgiving. The office is only open Monday and Tuesday. That means I'm really only out three days this week and two days the next."

Gina's assistant, who'd worked for her for the past six months and was only a year out of college, nodded enthusiastically. Like Gina, she dressed in stylish suits and great shoes. She was smart and eager to get ahead, reminding Gina of herself at that age—of herself to this day.

"I'm excited about this challenge," Carrie said.

Seeming satisfied, Kevin nodded and checked his Rolex. "I have a dinner meeting tonight with clients and I don't want to be late. I'll leave you two to hash over any details. What time does your plane leave, Gina?"

"Six a.m." Way too early, given that she'd probably get to bed around midnight tonight. But for more than a month now, she'd pretty much lived on sleep fumes. With the help of copious amounts of caffeine and plenty of chocolate, she'd managed just fine.

"You'll be back the Monday after Thanksgiving."

It was a statement, not a question. "That's right," Gina said.

She'd booked a return flight for that Sunday, giving her

ten full days in Montana. That should be enough time to see everyone and straighten out her uncle's affairs.

"Give my condolences to your family, and have a good holiday."

It wouldn't be much of a holiday. "Thank you, Kevin."

Her boss left.

Gina hadn't spent Thanksgiving or any other holiday with her relatives since her mother had died. They would probably expect her to cook Thanksgiving dinner, which was okay with her. She enjoyed cooking but never had the time anymore.

"Um, Gina?" Carrie said, bringing Gina back to the task at hand. "I'm meeting some friends in a little while and I should get going."

"Right," she said. "Let's review day by day what's supposed to happen between now and when I return. We'll start with Grant Industries and then go over the other accounts."

"I'm ready."

Carrie didn't quite manage to stifle a yawn, which caused Gina to yawn, too. They were both exhausted, but she needed to know she could depend on her assistant. A lot was riding on this campaign.

"This is a huge responsibility, Carrie. Are you sure you can handle it? Because I can easily bring in someone else." Several of her colleagues, including her best friend, Lise, would do anything for the Grant account. But when Grant Industries had signed with Andersen, Coats and Mueller, Kevin had selected Gina to manage it, and she preferred to keep Lise away from her "baby."

Carrie perked right up. "I'm thrilled to have this opportunity to prove myself."

Gina smiled, relieved. After reviewing all of their clients' accounts, Gina shut down her desktop computer.

"That's it, then. My uncle's ranch only has dial-up, but I found a hot spot for wireless so I'll be able to stay connected." She would have to drive about five miles into town to get internet, which was inconvenient but better than nothing.

"Seriously? No wireless?"

"Unfortunately not. My uncle was a rancher and didn't use the internet much. I expect frequent reports from you on the Grant account and the rest of our clients. Numbers, feedback plus any ideas or concerns you have. That way I can keep tabs on everything and make sure nothing slips through the cracks."

"No problem."

"Great. You have my cell phone number. If you need me for anything at all, text me or call—day or night. Oh, and Montana is an hour ahead of us, by the way."

Carrie nodded. "Don't worry about a thing, Gina. I can handle this."

Gina hoped she was right. Her job and her creditors depended on it.

DUSK WAS FALLING when Zach Horton exited Redd's battered Ford wagon. Icy wind blew across the airport parking lot, and he clapped his hand on his Stetson to keep it from flying across the pavement. Time to switch to a wool cap.

Redd blew on his gloved hands and squinted at the cloud-filled sky. "Looks like it's fixing to snow tonight. Good thing Gina's flight is due to arrive on time. I sure appreciate you driving my old heap to pick her up."

The seventy-one-year-old was too shaken up by his older brother's unexpected death to drive the forty miles to the airport alone, let alone in the dark. "I'm happy to help," Zach said. "I've been hearing about Lucky's niece since he hired me. It's time I met her."

She didn't know it, but Lucky had left her the ranch. He wanted her to take it over. Correction: he wanted Zach to persuade her to take it over. "Where did she say to meet her?" he asked.

"In the baggage claim area."

"She checked bags?"

"That's what she said."

Zach shrugged. According to Lucky, Gina Arnett was a marketing whiz, steadily climbing the corporate ladder. She'd recently been promoted to assistant vice president at her company. The whole family was proud of her.

Zach was familiar with the type. Uptight, driven, goal oriented—he'd had his fill of women like her. He'd had his fill of corporate deals and one-upmanships, period.

He doubted Gina Arnett would want anything to do with the Lucky A and had told Lucky so. But Lucky had asked Zach to do everything possible to persuade her. The rancher had taken Zach in when he was a broken man, and Zach owed him.

There weren't many people he counted as friends, and losing Lucky hurt. He would sorely miss the old man who had taken him in and mentored him in ways his own father never had.

He and Redd entered the baggage claim area, which was noisy and full of passengers awaiting their luggage.

After a moment, Redd pointed to a woman across the way. "There she is."

In high-heeled suede boots and a stylish camel hair coat over pants, she looked pretty much as Zach had pictured her, though taller. Her light brown hair was parted on the side and hung almost to her shoulders in a straight, sophisticated style. With big eyes, full lips and an air of self-confidence, she was knockout beautiful. Lucky had neglected to mention that.

"Uncle Redd," she said, hugging Redd tight. Her eyes flooded before she squeezed them shut.

Feeling like a voyeur, Zach stood back and averted his gaze, giving them privacy.

Finally, Redd let go of her and wiped his eyes. "Gina, this is Zach Horton—he's the foreman at the Lucky A."

She raised her watery gaze to Zach. Makeup had smeared under her grief-stricken eyes. For some reason, that made his chest hurt.

He whipped off his hat and extended his arm. "Pleased to meet you."

She had delicate fingers and a firm grip, her skin soft against his callused palm. "I'm sorry about Lucky," Zach said, sounding gruff to his own ears. He cleared his throat. "He talked about you quite a bit."

"He told me about you, too. I remember how happy he was when he hired you several years ago. He was always talking about how much he liked and respected you. I loved him so much." Her eyes filled.

As the tears spilled over, Zach's throat tightened, pressure building behind his own eyes. He turned away and nodded at the conveyor belt. "Here come the bags. Which one is yours?"

"I checked three—two big and one smaller. They're red with cream trim."

She was staying what? Ten days? This wasn't a vacation, and little Saddlers Prairie had only one real restaurant. What did she need all that stuff for? Zach didn't miss the laptop peeking out from her huge shoulder bag. She must be planning to work from the ranch. He'd expected that.

Gina pulled the smaller of the three bags from the conveyor belt and Zach grabbed the remaining two. Redd reached out to take one, but Zach shook his head. "Leave those to me."

"I'll take the other one, then." Redd pulled the smaller bag from Gina's grasp.

"Thank you both." She hooked her free arm through Redd's. They bowed their heads and made their way toward the exit.

SHIVERING, GINA TUCKED her cashmere scarf into her coat collar as she, Uncle Redd and Zach made their way toward her uncle's old station wagon. The icy Montana wind was every bit as biting as she remembered—not much different from Chicago in late November.

Snow flurries danced in the glow of the parking lot's perimeter lights. A few flakes could easily turn into a deluge, and she hoped they made it to the ranch while the roads were still passable.

"You sit in the front with Zach," Uncle Redd said, the breath puffing from his lips like smoke while Zach loaded the luggage into the cargo area.

Tired from lack of sleep and the long travel day, and feeling emotionally raw, Gina preferred to sit in the back and just be. "You take the front, Uncle Redd," she said. "I'm fine sitting in the back."

"That's where the dogs ride. You don't want to get dog hair on those pretty clothes."

He had a point.

Zach slammed the cargo door closed and headed toward the passenger side of the car. "Hop in," he said, opening the door for her.

He was big and muscular and movie-star good-looking, with a strong chin and wide forehead, and he was tall enough that even in boots with three-inch heels, she had to tip her head up to meet his gaze. She'd noticed his striking silvery-blue eyes halfway across the crowded baggage-claim area.

Despite her grief, and despite the fact that she was usually attracted to corporate-executive types, she was hyperaware of him.

What drew her most was the sorrow evident in his face. No one had expected her still-spry Uncle Lucky to die at seventy-four. His loss would no doubt be keenly felt by Zach and everyone in town.

She slid onto the bench-style front seat—Uncle Redd's car was that old. In an attempt to get warm, she hunched down and hugged herself.

Zach got into the driver's side with a fluid grace she hadn't expected of a man his size, shut his door and started the car. "Once the engine warms up, I'll turn the heat up high," he said.

As he rolled toward the exit, she glanced in the rearview mirror at her uncle. "I've missed Sugar and Bit. Are they still inseparable?"

"Pretty much. You'll see them at the house. If you want, you can keep them with you tonight for company. Wish I had the room at my place, but I don't."

The thought of staying alone at Uncle Lucky's didn't bother Gina. "Thanks, but your dogs won't even remember me. I'll be okay by myself."

"Probably better off without them." Uncle Redd chuckled. "Bit still thinks he's human, and that always gets Sugar's goat. They're like an old married couple."

"Sort of like Gloria and Sophie?" Gina teased. Her elderly cousins, widowed sisters, lived together and bickered constantly.

"Exactly, and almost as old in dog years. Bit's almost

ten and Sugar just turned nine." Redd sighed. "We're all gettin' up there—present company excluded."

"Don't forget, I recently turned thirty," Gina said. "That's not so young."

Zach made a sound that could've been a laugh. "You're just a kid."

She scoffed. "You can't be much older than me."

"Four years. That may not seem like a big difference, but trust me, I've been around the block a lot more than you have."

"I'm not exactly naive," she argued.

"From where I sit, you're both still babies," Uncle Redd quipped from the back.

Gina shared a look with Zach, both of them acknowledging that today, they felt old and weary.

At last Zach cranked up the heat, and a welcome blast of warm air hit Gina. The highway was dark and deserted, with only the car headlights lighting the way. No one spoke. The combination of warm air, darkness, silence and exhaustion was impossible to resist. Gina's eyes drifted shut. She was almost asleep when Uncle Redd broke the silence.

"Gina grew up here."

Zach glanced at her, his face shadowed in the dash lights. "Lucky said that after you graduated from high school, you left town."

She remembered that day well. Her parents had both been alive then, and excited about her future, yet sad to see her go. She'd been the opposite—desperate to leave Saddlers Prairie, get her education and start fresh in a big city. All her life, her parents had fought about money and struggled to make ends meet. From the time she was in grade school, Gina had vowed to leave town someday and find a high-paying job. She had no interest in ever coming back, except for occasional visits.

"She's the first one in our family to graduate college, let alone earn a master's degree," Uncle Redd said with pride. "She's a smart one and pretty, too."

"Uncle Redd!" Gina said, embarrassed.

"Well, you are."

She snuck a glance at Zach. His gaze never left the road, but his lips twitched, and she thought he might even crack a smile.

"Since the day she left she hasn't been back to visit but three times," Uncle Redd went on. "Once over Christmas break that first year in college and again when her dad— my oldest brother, Beau—passed that summer. After that, we didn't see her for another four years, when her mama took sick with pneumonia. Marie was forty-two when she had Gina. She and Beau had been married almost twenty years and didn't think they'd ever have kids. When Gina came along, they were over the moon. We all were. Of the three of us brothers, Beau was the only one to have a child."

"You don't need to bore Zach with all that," Gina said.

"I don't mind." Zach glanced at her. "I knew you were the only kid in the family, but Lucky didn't tell me the rest."

After another stretch of silence, Uncle Redd let out a loud yawn. Soon, soft snores floated from the backseat.

Gina glanced behind her. "He's out cold."

"I don't think he slept much last night." Zach rolled his shoulders as if he, too, were tired. "You're in marketing, right?"

She nodded. "I'm an assistant vice president with Andersen, Coats and Mueller."

"That's a big firm."

"You've heard of them?"

"I've read a few articles where they were mentioned. Do you like what you do?"

No one had ever asked her that, and she had to stop and think. "I love it."

That wasn't quite true. She loved the perks that put her in contact with the decision makers in big and small companies, and she liked the respect from her boss, colleagues, family and friends. "It's hard work, though. Right now, I'm in the middle of holiday campaigns for several clients." Her turn to yawn. "It seems like weeks since I've had a decent night's sleep."

Even without the holiday push, she couldn't remember the last time she'd slept through the night.

"Let me guess—you live on caffeine."

"And chocolate. Lots of both."

"And you enjoy living that way?"

"The chocolate part, for sure." She smiled. "Everyone knows that if you want to get ahead, you have to work long hours."

Although Zach didn't comment, Gina had the feeling he wasn't impressed. She wanted him to understand.

"Growing up, we had enough to eat and a roof over our heads, but we were poor," she said. "My maternal grandfather owned a farm equipment business, and when my parents married, he hired my dad to work for him. Then, when my grandfather died, my dad took over the company. For some reason it never did very well. My mother worked two jobs to pay the bills. I always wanted something better."

"That makes sense. So do you have the life you want?"

She was getting there. "I own a condo in an upscale high-rise and I drive a Lexus." Between the steep mortgage, car payments and credit-card bills, she never quite made ends meet, but that was her business. "I can eat out wherever I please and buy new clothes anytime I want. You draw your own conclusions."

"Sounds as if you're doing well."

A few moments of uncomfortable silence filled the car. Gina searched her mind for something else to talk about.

"Where are you from, Zach?"

"Houston."

"I thought I heard a bit of the South in your voice."

She was about to ask about his background and what had brought him to Saddlers Prairie when he turned on the radio. A Carrie Underwood song filled the air. And with that, the conversation was over.

Gina shifted so that she faced the passenger window. Giving in to the exhaustion weighting her down, she closed her eyes.

She didn't wake up until Zach shut off the engine and touched her shoulder. "Wake up, Gina. We're here."

## Chapter Two

Zach gathered with the entire Arnett family, dogs included, in the living room of Lucky's house. They'd asked him to help play host to a steady stream of visitors, including the four members of the ranch crew and their families who stayed on during winter.

Lucky hadn't even been dead forty-eight hours, but that didn't stop the well-meaning townspeople. They brought food, offered solace and shared stories about the old rancher.

A cheerful fire danced in the fireplace, at odds with the occasion, and the little room was almost too warm. None of the Arnetts seemed to mind the heat or the company. Zach was grateful for the support and for their acceptance of him, no questions asked. It was a good thing because he wasn't about to air his dirty laundry to anyone. Only Lucky had known the truth.

From that first day Zach had drifted into town nearly three years ago, lost and broken, the people of Saddlers Prairie had welcomed him. Zach hadn't planned on staying, had only known that he needed to get out of Houston and start fresh someplace else. The big sky, rolling prairies and wide-open spaces of Montana had appealed to him, and the welcome mat in Saddlers Prairie had pulled him in.

In need of money—he was damned if he'd touch his bank account—he'd applied for work at the Lucky A. He hadn't known squat about ranching, but Lucky had taken a chance on him and offered him a job. Wanting the rancher to know what kind of man he was first, Zach had told him the whole sorry story of the commercial real-estate company he'd built and his subsequent downfall, sparing none of the ugly details.

Lucky had accepted him anyway and advised him to put the past behind him. Zach had done just that. He'd learned the ranching business and had soon become Lucky's foreman. The successful CEO he'd once been and the beautiful woman he'd been engaged to seemed like part of someone else's life.

Clay Hollyer, also a transplant and a former bull-riding champion who now worked as a rancher supplying stock to rodeos around the West, wandered toward Zach. His pretty wife, Sarah, pregnant with their first child, was at his side.

The couple offered their condolences. "What will you do now?" Clay asked.

The near future was a no-brainer. "Someone needs to take care of the ranch, so I'll be staying at the Lucky A for a while."

After that, Zach had no idea—except that he wanted to stay in town. His father and stepmother thought he was out of his mind for living in a trailer on a run-down ranch and working for peanuts when he didn't have to. But Zach had learned to draw happiness from the little things in life and, for now, he was content.

He glanced around for Gina. She was standing to the side of the fireplace, beautiful and animated as she chatted with people.

Make that he *used* to be content.

Now that Zach had met Gina, keeping his promise to Lucky and convincing her to hold on to the Lucky A seemed even more of a Sisyphean task than he'd thought. He seriously doubted that Gina would give up her career to run the Lucky A, but if he could at least convince her to keep the ranch in the family... That was what Lucky really wanted, for her to pass it down to her heirs—that was, if she had children one day.

She seemed so driven that Zach didn't know if she wanted kids. She sure was good with Bit and Sugar, though. The two dogs seemed wild about her, too. Bit, a Jack Russell, pranced around her, and Sugar, a white, sixty-pound husky, wagged her tail nonstop. Both of them hovered close and gazed at her adoringly, which said something about her.

Locals and transplants seemed to want to be around her, too. A group of women, some of whom she'd probably known growing up, surrounded her. Among them were Meg Dawson and her sister-in-law, Jenny Dawson, and Autumn Naylor, who were all married to ranchers, and Stacy Engle, who was the wife of Dr. Mark Engle, the sole doctor in Saddlers Prairie.

As engaged as Gina appeared to be, Zach noticed her yawn a few times. After spending the whole day traveling, she had to be exhausted. It had been a tough couple of days, and Zach fought the drowsies himself. Without thinking about it, he moved toward her. Her friends offered condolences to Zach before wandering off.

"You doing okay?" he asked, leaning in close to be heard over the noise in the room. He caught a whiff of perfume, something sweet and floral that reminded him of hot tropical nights.

"I'm managing. I found out from Stacy that you're

the one who found Uncle Lucky yesterday. What exactly happened?"

Zach didn't like talking about it. "Lucky was supposed to meet me at the back pasture first thing in the morning. When he didn't show and didn't answer his phone, I came here, to the house, looking for him."

"And you found him still in bed. Uncle Redd mentioned that Uncle Lucky had a heart attack, but he didn't tell me about you finding him." Gina shuddered. "That must've been awful."

"Not the best way to start your day." Zach grimaced. "The only good part of it is knowing that Lucky was asleep when he died and didn't suffer. We should all be so lucky."

"Pun intended?" she asked, her mouth hinting at a smile.

"No, but what the heck." Zach grinned.

He liked Gina. He couldn't help himself. Not just because she was easy to look at. She also cared about her family and the people in this house. They seemed genuinely pleased to see her, and she acted as if the feeling was mutual.

She fit in well here. She *belonged*. Did she know how special that was?

"Do you ever see yourself moving back to Saddlers Prairie?" he asked, feeling her out.

"Are you kidding?" She let out a humorless laugh. "I'm staying through Thanksgiving, period. One week from Sunday, I'll be on a flight back to Chicago. I hope—"

"I'm glad you two are getting a chance to know each other," Gina's cousin Gloria said as she and her sister Sophie squeezed past several people to join the two of them.

Both gray haired with sharp, brown eyes, their faces

looked so much alike, they could've been twins. That was where the resemblance stopped.

Gloria, bigger boned and taller than Sophie by a good four inches, patted his arm. "Isn't Zach wonderful?"

Sophie, who was two years younger than Gloria and soft around the middle, fluttered her lashes at him. "I hope you're getting enough to eat, Zach. There's a ton more food in the kitchen."

"I've had a plate or two, thanks."

"That's good." Sophie turned to Gina with a fond smile. "You're so thin, cookie. Did you eat?"

"I've been nibbling." Gina yawned.

Gloria gave her sister a dirty look. "You don't look too thin to me, sweetie. You're just right. Tomorrow will be a busy day. You have an early afternoon meeting with Matt Granger, Lucky's attorney. He'll give you a list of errands like you had had when your mother passed—stopping at the bank and so forth. You'll also want to make calls to cancel Lucky's health insurance and Social Security, any subscriptions he had and who knows what else."

Sophie frowned. "Don't burden her with all that now. She's exhausted, aren't you, cookie?" She grinned at Zach. "I call her 'cookie' because I could just eat her up!"

"You'll eat anything," Gloria muttered. "Land sakes, Sophie, she isn't a child anymore."

Used to the bickering, Zach glanced at Gina and saw her smother a smile.

"Now, now," Gina soothed, hooking her arms through her elderly cousins'. "Remember what's happened. And don't refer to me in the third person."

"All right, sweetie. Excuse us a moment, Zach." Gloria pulled Gina away from Sophie, speaking loudly enough that anyone within ten feet could hear. "What I was try- ing to say before *she*—" Gloria jerked her chin Sophie's way "—so rudely interrupted, is that tomorrow you'll be going nonstop, and you should probably get some sleep."

"We have guests, and I don't want to be rude."

"Yes, but you traveled all day, and it's an hour later in Chicago. People will understand, and they all know they'll see you again at the funeral. Zach and the rest of us will hold down the fort."

Sophie nodded. "We made up the guest bedroom you always use and put fresh towels in the bathroom for you." She lowered her voice. "Don't worry about Lucky's bedding. We disposed of it, so you won't have to. We wish you could stay with us, but we don't have the room. Unless you want to sleep on the living room couch…"

"I'll be fine," she said. "I think I will go upstairs in a minute."

After saying good-night to everyone and exchanging hugs and tears, she bent down to pat the dogs. They licked her and then trotted over to Uncle Redd.

"Thanks again for picking me up tonight," she told Zach. "I worried about Uncle Redd driving all that way, especially in the dark. I offered to rent a car, but you know how stubborn he is."

"Stubbornness seems to be an Arnett family trait." Zach's mouth quirked again, and Gina smiled. "If you can't sleep tonight and need company, give me a call. My trailer is just across the ranch."

"Good to know, but I'm so tired I'll probably fall asleep the second my head hits the pillow. Although if we didn't have a houseful of guests tonight, I'd take Uncle Redd's car and drive to the hotspot near the post office and check my email, just to make sure my assistant survived without me today." Gina yawned so hard, her eyes watered. "She hasn't called, so I guess she did. I'll call her in the morning."

Zach thought about telling her to blow off work and take care of herself instead, but he doubted she'd listen. He ought to know—three years ago, he'd been just like her. Probably even worse.

He nodded. "Sleep tight."

"And don't let the bedbugs bite? When I was a little girl, Uncle Lucky used to say that when I spent the night here. Good night, Zach."

He watched her trudge up the stairs, moving as if she was beyond weary. It was going to be a rough ten days.

USED TO WAKING up early, Gina opened her eyes after a sound sleep. At first she had no idea where she was. It was still dark outside, but she could make out the faded curtains and old blinds pulled over the window and feel the lumpy mattress. She was in the small, plain guestroom she thought of as hers at Uncle Lucky's ranch.

But Uncle Lucky was gone.

Bleary-eyed but feeling oddly rested, she stumbled out of bed. The chattering of the guests downstairs had lulled her to sleep, and she had actually slept though the night. No tossing and turning, no waking up and worrying. Which was surprising, but Gina wasn't going to question her good luck.

She peered through the blinds. Sometime during the night, a few inches of snow had fallen. It wasn't enough to cause problems, but it blanketed the rolling fields in white.

Uncle Lucky's house was old and outdated, but thanks to storm windows and a working furnace, it was reasonably warm. So different from Gina's childhood home, where winters meant shivering from the second she crawled out of bed until she climbed back in under the covers at night.

It wasn't exactly the Ritz here, but at least everything

was in working order. Uncle Redd could move in without doing any repairs or updates, which would suit him fine. None of the Arnetts enjoyed spending money without a good reason. Gina had a very good reason for spending hers—to be successful, she had to look the part.

Still in a sleep fog, she padded to the bathroom. A shower helped shake out the cobwebs, and once she fixed her hair and applied makeup, she felt much better. Knowing she would be meeting with the attorney that afternoon and not wanting to have to change clothes later, she dressed in a cream cashmere sweater set and gray slacks, a stunning outfit purchased on credit at Neiman Marcus. Sliding her feet into her slippers, she headed downstairs.

Now that the visitors had all left, the little house was eerily silent. Much too quiet, but at the moment, Gina's main concern was coffee.

As a child, she'd spent every summer here, and she knew her way around her uncle's cluttered kitchen. Now cakes, pies and breads filled every spare bit of counter space, but some kind soul had cleaned up last night and run Uncle Lucky's portable dishwasher. Gina unhooked it from the faucet and wheeled it to its place against the wall, bypassing a stack of old newspapers that probably went back five years. Those had to go, but not just now. Coffee. She needed coffee.

Uncle Lucky had always preferred the no-frills stuff, and his coffeemaker was the kind that percolated on the stove and took its sweet time. Compared to the state-of-the-art coffee and espresso maker at Gina's condo, it seemed primitive.

Not that she made her own coffee often. In Chicago, she could run down the street and pick up an espresso at any number of places. But Saddlers Prairie didn't have many options. Barb's Café was nearly a five-mile drive from the ranch, and the Burger Palace, a fast-food place, was almost ten. Neither was open for business this early. She was stuck with Uncle Lucky's generic brand.

While the coffee brewed, Gina cut herself a thick slab of cinnamon-raisin bread. She popped it into the toaster and waited. Without Wi-Fi, she wasn't able to check her email and felt lost. She did have a text from Carrie. The rollout of the Grant Holiday Magic campaign had gone as smoothly as Gina had hoped, which was good news. Carrie didn't mention the other clients, and Gina assumed that all was well.

Her assistant's personal news was interesting. She texted she'd gone with friends to a bar after work on Tuesday and had met someone. He'd asked her to go out for dinner with him on Wednesday, and she had been about to leave for her date as soon as she fired off the report with the campaign's numbers. Gina would stop at the Wi-Fi hotspot and read the report later.

At least one of them was dating. Gina texted back a thanks for the info and asked about the dinner date.

She didn't need to talk to her assistant this morning, but she was used to being busy all the time, and the lack of rushing around and accomplishing things was unnerving. She dialed the office.

"Hi, Marsha, it's Gina," she told the receptionist. "Please put me through to Carrie."

"She hasn't come in yet."

Gina checked her watch. It was after nine in Chicago, well past time to start the workday. "Where is she?"

"Well, she had that dinner date last night. Maybe she stayed out late and overslept."

Not a good sign.

"Wait, I just remembered something," Marsha said. "On her way out last night, she mentioned something about stopping at some of the Grant department stores today. Maybe she's at a store right now."

Conducting a visual check. That made sense. Gina let out a relieved breath—and then wondered what she had been worried about. Carrie was a younger version of herself. As eager as she was to move up the corporate ladder, she wouldn't blow this.

"I've been thinking about you and your family," Marsha said with sympathy. "How are you doing?"

"It's not easy, but I'm managing," she said and gave Marsha a few details. "Will you have Carrie call me when she comes in?"

Gina disconnected and made a mental list of what she needed to do this morning. She would start with compiling Uncle Lucky's bank statements and legal documents so that she could take them to the meeting with the attorney. Her uncle's office was even more cluttered than the kitchen, and finding what she needed wouldn't be easy.

She also thought about the funeral tomorrow and all that entailed. Her family expected her to give the eulogy, which she'd started to write in bed last night. Gina didn't plan on taking up too much time because other people also planned to speak, but she still needed to hone her speech and practice it.

At some point she needed to sort through the old papers and junk her uncle had collected. And he'd collected piles of both.

Suddenly, she felt even more tired than she had yesterday. Last night, more than a few people had offered to help her with whatever she needed. After she sorted through everything, she would take some of them up on the offer and ask for help hauling things to the dump or the nearest charity bin.

For now, clearing out the clutter would keep her busy.

At last, the coffee was ready. It didn't smell very good, but beggars couldn't be choosers. She filled a chipped mug and searched the aging fridge for milk.

Casseroles, cheese plates and all kinds of food crammed the shelves. Thanks to the kind people of Saddlers Prairie, there was enough food in there to feed a small army. Even with Uncle Redd, Gloria and Sophie helping her eat it, there were enough meals to last until Thanksgiving.

She took her buttered toast and coffee to the table and sat down. Maybe Zach would help them eat some of this stuff.

Zach. Now there was a man. He was big and super good-looking—every girl's dream cowboy.

Gina frowned and reminded herself that she wasn't into cowboys. She liked ambitious men in well-tailored suits. She hadn't met the right one yet, but she had no doubt that, in time, she would.

The coffee tasted awful. If she hadn't needed the caffeine so badly she'd dump it down the drain. She was revising her eulogy and picking at her toast when someone knocked at the back door.

Pathetically eager for company, she jumped up and hurried to open it. Zach stood on the stoop, his face ruddy from the cold. Against the backdrop of the blue sky, his hair looked almost black and his eyes were the color of liquid silver. His heavy parka was unzipped, revealing a flannel shirt tucked into jeans.

"Morning," he said, his breath fogging in the cold air. "I finished the chores and thought you might want company."

How had he known?

"Sure." She widened the door. "Come in."

After wiping his boots on the mat he stepped inside,

bringing a whiff of fresh air with him. "It's cold out there," he said, blowing on his hands.

"It's nice and warm in here."

As Zach shrugged out of his parka and hung it on one of the hooks along the wall near the door, Gina couldn't help admiring his broad shoulders, narrow hips and long legs.

He caught her staring. His mouth quirked and he raised his eyebrows.

It was a good thing she didn't blush easily. "I was wondering whether I should offer you coffee," she said. "Lucky's coffeemaker is older than I am, and this stuff tastes pretty bad. But there's plenty to eat if you're hungry."

Zach glanced at what was left of her toast. "That looks good."

"I'll slice some for you."

She started to stand, but Zach gestured for her to stay seated. "Relax—I'll get it myself. I met the woman who made that bread when she brought it by yesterday. Her name is Cora Mullins, and she went to grade school with Lucky."

He pulled a plate from the cupboard as if he was family. From the way Uncle Lucky had sung his praises, she knew he'd thought of him that way.

"May as well try the coffee, too," he said, grabbing a mug.

A few minutes later, he joined her at the kitchen table. He sipped cautiously. "Compared to the sludge Lucky makes—made—this isn't half bad."

He made a face that coaxed a smile from Gina. "Believe me, I tasted his coffee several times," she said. "I'm surprised I didn't sprout hair on my chest."

Zach's gaze darted to her breasts. Interest flared in his

eyes and her body jumped to life. Maybe he wasn't her type, but she sure was attracted to him.

He glanced at her pad and paper. "Don't tell me you're working."

"I was trying to revise what I want to say at the funeral." She bit her lip. "But thinking about that makes me sad."

"Talk about Lucky's coffee. That'll get a smile out of everyone."

She hadn't thought of using humor. "Smiling through the tears—I like it."

Zach wolfed down the bread, obviously famished from whatever he'd been doing outside. "Before I forget, here's the key to Lucky's truck." He raised his hip and set the key and her uncle's rabbit foot keychain on the table. "He logged over a hundred and seventy thousand miles on it but maintained the engine beautifully. It runs great, but it's a stick shift and doesn't have power steering. Think you can handle that?"

She scoffed. "I learned to drive in that truck."

"No kidding! So Lucky gave you driving lessons?"

When she nodded, Zach shook his head and chuckled, a nice sound that brightened up the gray morning. "What's so funny?" she asked.

"The man was hell on wheels, pushing the truck so hard, it's a wonder he didn't burn up the engine he took such care with. I was picturing you with the pedal to the metal and the truck churning up clouds of dust. I'll bet Lucky got a big kick out of that."

"Especially when I pushed the speed up to sixty— which was about as fast as the old truck could go." She smiled at the memory. "I was fourteen, too young for a driver's license, but Uncle Lucky said I needed to learn in case of an emergency. He took me out on a few deserted roads where the sheriff wouldn't spot us and there were no other cars for me to hit.

"I spent most every summer with him while my parents worked at fairs around the state, trying to drum up business," she added.

"I'm surprised your dad didn't want to ranch."

"He, Uncle Lucky and Uncle Redd grew up on the Lucky A, but only Uncle Lucky stayed. Uncle Redd left to run the agricultural department of Spenser's General Store, and my dad went to work at my grandfather's farm equipment business. He said he liked getting paid regularly, but I don't remember that ever happening. But I mentioned that the other night."

"Yeah. That must've been tough."

"I was born into it, so I didn't know any better. But my parents did, and their money troubles definitely took a toll on their marriage." Gina didn't like to think of those times. "That's why I left home and why I work so hard at my job."

For no reason at all, her eyes teared up.

The concerned look Zach gave her only made her feel worse. "You miss him, don't you?"

She nodded and tried to blink back the tears. In vain.

"Uncle Lucky kept asking me to come back and visit," she said. "He said he had something to say to me in person. Now it's too late, and I'll never know what it was. Why didn't I make the time to come back?"

# Chapter Three

Gina hunched her shoulders and wiped her eyes, and it was obvious that she was racked with guilt for not visiting while Lucky was still alive. She also seemed tormented over not knowing what he'd wanted to tell her. Zach knew, and this seemed a good time to enlighten her.

Even now she was beautiful, her eyes a soft green through the bright sheen of tears. She bit her bottom lip, and then freed it. Full again, it looked pink and soft and warm....

Zach tore his gaze away. He had a job to do, and he wasn't going to think about his strong attraction to her. She was mired in the corporate world and he wanted to stay as far away from that as possible.

He handed her a paper napkin to blow her nose. "Don't beat yourself up over what you can't change," he said, giving her the same advice Lucky had given him. "Your uncle knew you loved him, and that's what counts."

"But I'll never know what he wanted to talk to me about." She brushed crumbs from the tabletop into her hand and dumped them on her plate.

"I think I do."

"Oh? Tell me."

Her mouth opened a fraction, and from out of nowhere, Zach had the crazy urge to taste those lips. *Down, boy.*

He raised his gaze and gave her a level look. "Lucky wanted to talk to you about his decision to leave you the Lucky A."

She blinked in surprise. "That can't be right. Uncle Redd is his brother. The ranch is supposed go to him."

"Lucky and Redd discussed it, and they both felt it should pass to you."

"But Uncle Redd never said a word about that over the phone or last night. I think you misunderstood."

Having sat in on the conversation, Zach shook his head. "I know what I'm talking about, but if you don't believe me, you'll find out when you meet with Matt Granger this afternoon."

"But I don't want this ranch," Gina said, looking stricken.

"All the same, it's yours."

"What am I supposed to do with it?"

Zach figured that was a rhetorical question, and in the silent moment that passed, he could almost see her mind work—and it worked fast.

"I guess I'll sell it," she said.

Not if Zach could stop her. "That's one option, but Lucky wants—wanted—to keep it in the family."

"Then he shouldn't have left it to me," she muttered, pushing her hair behind her ears. "I've had a lot of good times here, but I saw my uncle struggle every year. I know how hard it is to work from dawn to dusk, sometimes longer, all the while praying that Mother Nature behaves so that you can make a profit and survive another year. Sorry, but I'll pass."

She wore a stubborn look that reminded Zach of Lucky. With that and the defiant lift of her chin, Zach knew she'd made up her mind. Still, he had a promise to keep. "At least think about it for a few days. For Lucky."

"You're playing the guilt card. That isn't fair." Once again, she caught her lip between her teeth. "Even if I wanted to keep the ranch, and believe me, I don't, I don't see how that's possible. I live in Chicago. That's where my job—my life—is, and where I want to be. I'm a city girl now. Lucky's known for years that I wasn't coming back here."

"He left you the ranch anyway." Zach let the words hang there for a moment. "Ranching is good, honest work," he added.

"And for the most part, ranchers are good people—I know that. But it doesn't pay, not for the Lucky A. I don't have to look at my uncle's bank statement to know that he doesn't have two dimes to his name. He always struggled to keep his head above water. I decided long ago that this wasn't the life for me."

"Lucky used to talk about how you helped with the chores around here and how you enjoyed taking care of the animals and being outside."

"When I was little, I did."

Zach tried a different tack. "Can you honestly say you're happy with your life?"

"What are you, my psychiatrist?" she quipped, but she looked like a deer in headlights. "I'm a creative person, and I get to use that creativity in my work."

She hadn't answered the question, which in itself was an answer. "You didn't look like you were being creative when you walked off the plane last night," Zach said. "You looked ready to drop."

"I don't mind the long hours because it means that I'm successful and productive. And FYI, I happen to thrive on stress and a big workload."

Having been there, Zach understood. He also knew that

that kind of adrenaline never resulted in long-term satisfaction. "So you enjoy life on the human hamster wheel."

"Sometimes it does seem like that, but… You couldn't possibly understand."

"Because I'm a ranch foreman." Stung, Zach crossed his arms. "You don't know anything about what I understand. You don't know anything about *me*." He considered explaining about the company he'd once owned, the things he'd done for the bottom line and the terrible price he'd paid. But that was his business. Besides, it was behind him now.

The starch went out of her spine. "That was rude, and I apologize."

Zach nodded. She angled her head and really looked at him. "You're right. I know very little about you, except that you're from Houston. There are ranches all over Texas. How did you end up at the Lucky A in Saddlers Prairie, Montana?"

"I needed a change." Which was all he was going to say. "You should know that I made a promise to Lucky that I'd convince you to keep the ranch."

"You're trying to change the subject. Don't tell me— you left Houston because you're a criminal." Her eyebrows arched and her eyes twinkled, lighting her whole face.

"Very funny. Nope." Not directly, anyway. In his own eyes, he was. The family of Sam Swain, the man who'd suffered a heart attack and died after Zach had forged the business deal that had undercut what he wanted, probably agreed. But Zach's family and fiancée at the time hadn't believed he'd done anything wrong—except when he'd sold his own company.

"You're going to have to break your promise to Lucky. I can't possibly—"

Not wanting to hear it, Zach held up his hands, palms out. "Just listen."

She sighed. "All right, but I've made up my mind."

"You no doubt know that people all over the country, maybe even the world, romanticize cowboys and ranching. Some even dream of living the ranching life. Why not indulge in that dream by offering a working vacation on a ranch?"

"You're talking about a dude ranch." She was tuned in now, her eyes bright and interested.

"Exactly. A few months ago, Lucky and I started laying out plans for turning the Lucky A into a working dude ranch. Imagine visitors staying for a weekend or as long as two weeks, paying for 'the ranching experience,'" he said, making air quotes, "and providing free labor. In return, the Lucky A supplies lodging, meals and expertise."

"Uncle Lucky thought that up?" Gina looked confused.

"Actually, I did, but Lucky jumped at the idea, especially after we penciled out the numbers. We'd have to update the bunkhouse and hire a cook, but if we brought in just twenty people a month between May and October, we'd break even."

"My uncle has never penciled out numbers for anything." Gina gave him a shrewd look. "Something tells me you haven't always been a ranch foreman."

"I've dabbled in a few other things. What do you think about the Lucky A Dude Ranch?"

"I have questions. These days, the crew lives in trailers. The bunkhouse hasn't been used for years, except for storage. Getting it in working order will take a lot of updating. Where does the money to make those improvements come from?"

"We penciled that out, too. The wiring and plumbing are in decent enough shape, but the building needs more insulation and a new furnace and air conditioner, plus paint and new fixtures. I can do everything but install the heating and cooling systems, which will save a bundle. The estimated cost will be roughly twenty to thirty thousand dollars."

"That's a lot of money."

Zach put up his hand, palm out, to silence her. "Lucky and I talked to the bank and they were willing to loan him half of that. If beef prices stay high, we figured he'd net the rest by spring. Once the business is up and running and profitable and the loan is paid back, we'll look into adding a couple of cabins."

Gina stacked her mug on top of her empty plate. "As intriguing as the idea is, you can count me out."

He'd expected this. "You say that now, but I'm not giving up." He scraped his chair back and stood. "Thanks for the coffee and toast. Before I forget, the combination to your uncle's safe is his dad's birthday, April 5, zero four zero five one nine. I'll let myself out."

He left her sitting at the table.

THAT AFTERNOON, ZACH, Curly and Bert, two of the crew members, checked the water troughs that provided a steady supply of water to the cattle. Sometime during the night, the heater in the big water tank had failed and the water had frozen in the pipes. Thirsty cattle had ventured onto the ice at the river, which was slippery and dangerous. Pete, a mechanical whiz, was already at work repairing the heater.

Donning safety glasses, the three of them wielded shovels and pickaxes to break the stuff up in the troughs and remove it. Then, with the help of a blowtorch, they began to melt the water in the pipes. For now the cattle would have the water they needed.

They were almost finished when Zach's cell phone rang. He pulled off a glove and slid the phone from his jacket pocket. He didn't recognize the number, but the 312 area code was Chicago's. Had to be Gina.

He'd been thinking about her pretty much nonstop since that morning. Everything about her both fascinated and irritated him. The cute expression on her face when she told him about the awful coffee she'd made, her pretty smile and the way her eyes had sparked when she defended her career. How her breasts had looked in that sweater.

Zach swallowed. He was way too attracted to her for his own good and was both pleased that she had his number and put out that she'd called.

Curly and Bert eyed him curiously.

"I better get this," he said. "This is Zach," he answered gruffly.

A slight hesitation. Then, "It's Gina. Is this a bad time to call?"

Did she have any idea of the knots she'd tied him up in? Yeah, it was a bad time. "I thought you had to meet with Matt Granger," he said, drawing raised eyebrows from Curly. He knew that Granger was Lucky's lawyer and realized who Zach was talking with. After hearing about her from Lucky for years, the crew had finally met her at the house last night.

"I'm supposed to meet him at three, but I can't find Uncle Lucky's bank receipts or other papers. I thought I'd find them in his desk, but they aren't there. Uncle Redd isn't answering his phone, and neither is Gloria or Sophie."

"Did you check the safe?"

"Um, I don't know where it is."

Why hadn't she asked him this morning? As much as Zach trusted the two crew members, he wasn't about to tell her within hearing range of them. "Hang on a sec." He muted his end of the line so she couldn't hear him. "I need to go to the house and help Gina with something."

"I'll bet you do," Bert said, giving him a sly look. "She's a foxy one."

Zach narrowed his eyes, and the burly ranch hand backed up a step. "No offense meant. What do you want us to do when we finish here?"

"Help Chet with loading the hay onto the flatbed. Make sure none of the herd has wandered off, and feed and water the horses. If you run into problems, give me a call."

Zach climbed into his truck and drove to the house.

Looking worried, Gina met him at the back door. "I had to call the attorney and reschedule for four. I can't find anything in the desk except junk. Uncle Lucky is— was—such a pack rat."

Zach eyed the four-foot-high stack of yellowing news-papers against the kitchen wall. "He sure was." He wiped his feet and stepped inside. "So you don't know where the safe is."

"I didn't even know he had one until you mentioned it this morning, and I thought…I assumed that the papers I needed would be in the desk."

"Let's go into Lucky's office." Zach followed Gina through the kitchen and down the hallway. She was wear-ing the same sexy sweater and pants as that morning, an outfit that had to cost a mint. Gina had a great ass and hips that swayed naturally and seductively.

By the time they reached the office, he was semi-hard and not happy about that. Turning away from her, he headed through the room, stopping in front of an oil painting of a cowboy astride a horse that hung opposite the desk. He lifted the painting off the wall and set it carefully down.

Gina's eyes widened. "For as long as I can remember, that painting has been hanging there. I had no idea it was hiding a safe."

"Now you know. This is where you'll find all of Lucky's important papers, including a copy of the will and our spreadsheet for the dude ranch."

"See, a word like *spreadsheet*—that wasn't part of my uncle's vocabulary."

"After we developed one, it was. Try the combination." Zach stepped back so that she could work the numbers.

She opened the safe and pulled out half a dozen folders. There was no room for them on Lucky's cluttered desk, so she stacked them on the desk chair. "Just look at all this stuff."

She was definitely unhappy about her uncle's filing system. A lock of hair had fallen over her eyes, but she didn't seem to notice.

"I wish I'd started earlier," she said. "I'm not going to have time to look through everything, so I guess I'll bring all these folders with me. Thanks for stopping what you were doing and showing me the safe, Zach. I don't know what I'd have done otherwise."

"Helping you out is part of my job."

She tugged at her sweater, drawing his gaze to her breasts. "I've been thinking about how we left things this morning. You meant a lot to Lucky, and he obviously trusted you. You're important to this ranch. My family and I need you here, Zach. You're not going to quit, are you?"

"I wouldn't do that. But you should know that I intend to honor my promise to Lucky. I'll do what I can to change your mind."

"Try away. It won't work."

With her chin up and the confident smile on her mouth, she was irresistible.

"That sounds like a challenge—and I always like challenges," he said, advancing toward her. "Did you mean that?"

"I... Did I mean what?"

"About me trying to convince you." Her eyes were the prettiest color, green with little flecks of brown and gold. "Did you?"

He brushed the silky lock back from her face and tucked it behind her ear. Her pupils dilated and he knew she felt some of what he did. She touched her lips with the tip of her tongue in what he recognized as a nervous gesture.

"I—"

He laid his finger over her soft lips. "Shhh." Tipping up her chin, he kissed her.

ZACH'S HANDS WERE cold from being outside, but his lips were warm. And very good at their job. Gina hadn't kissed anyone since she and Wayne had parted ways in June. Even in their first few months together, when there was some degree of passion between them, Wayne had never kissed her like this.

The kiss was firm, yet sweet and gentle, and something more she couldn't define. Whatever it was, she liked it. A lot. Zach smelled of fresh air and man and was every bit as hard and muscled as he looked.

His arms tightened around her, and she willingly sank against him. Another kiss followed, and another. Shifting so that she was even closer, he slid his tongue over hers. Gina felt his arousal against her stomach. Her nipples tingled and her panties were instantly damp.

She wanted to go on kissing him forever. Instead she pushed him away.

He looked every bit as stunned by the heat between

them as she was. "You better go or you'll be even later for your meeting," he said, his eyes hot as he straightened her sweater.

"Right." She managed to close the safe and hang the painting with barely a tremble.

"You're a very convincing man," she murmured on the way to the kitchen. "But—"

"You're still going to sell."

She nodded.

By the time they reached the back door, she felt reasonably normal again. "Thanks," she said as she opened the door for him.

The corner of his mouth lifted. "For showing you the safe, or for those kisses?"

Both. "I'll see you later."

"No doubt. Have fun with the lawyer."

In a daze, Gina drove down the highway in Uncle Lucky's hulking truck. Traffic was light, but then in Saddlers Prairie it always was. Her mind wandered. She couldn't get over Zach's kissing her and how much she'd enjoyed it. In Uncle Lucky's office of all places.

Her uncle had only been gone a few days. They hadn't even held the funeral yet, and here she was fantasizing about the hunky foreman. What was she thinking?

That was the trouble—she hadn't thought at all. She'd simply reacted. Boy, had she.

Up in rancher heaven, Uncle Lucky was probably shaking his head, wondering if she'd lost her mind.

She had—temporarily. Zach Horton wasn't her type. Besides, she wouldn't be here long. Getting involved with him was a bad idea.

Involved? Gina frowned. Just where had that idea come from? So they'd shared a few kisses. Fabulous, bone-melting kisses, the thought of which, even now, made her lips tingle and her stomach flutter. They didn't mean anything and wouldn't happen again.

Though if Zach did kiss her again, she wasn't at all sure she'd stop him.

Her cell phone rang. Grateful for the interruption and eager to get her mind off Zach and his kisses, she set her phone on speaker mode and picked up.

"It's Carrie," her assistant said.

Gina started guiltily. She hadn't thought about work or Carrie since early this morning. "It's about time you called me back," she chided. "Where have you been all day?"

"Where do you think I've been?" Carrie sounded defensive.

"I called you early this morning—hours ago."

"The note from Marsha didn't say it was urgent. Did she tell you that I was at the office until almost nine-thirty last night? I was up before dawn this morning and worked from home. Then I stopped in at a few of the Grant stores so that I could get a visual to go with the numbers they've been sharing." She filled Gina in on what she'd observed. "I sent you an email with all the details. Did you see it?"

"Not yet, but I'll be checking soon." On the way back from the attorney's office.

Things seemed to be going well, and Gina smiled. "That sounds good, Carrie. I'm impressed with what you've done. I thought you were supposed to have dinner last night with that guy you met at the bar."

"Chad. Yeah, but it was too late for dinner, so we had drinks instead. We made a dinner date for this weekend."

Been there, done that. Getting ahead sometimes meant putting your personal life on hold. "I'm glad he's flexible," Gina said.

"Chad's an attorney—he understands long hours. That's one of the many things we have in common."

Everything Carrie said reminded Gina of herself and Wayne. When they'd first started dating they'd both thought they shared a number of interests. But after a few months, they'd realized that the only thing they really had in common was the desire to climb the corporate ladder. Neither of them had been upset when they'd parted ways.

"Have you had a chance to work on any of our other campaigns?" Gina asked. "Is there anything I should know about?"

She heard the sound of papers shuffling. "Oh, you know—the usual reports and phone calls. All the companies are anxious about their holiday campaigns."

Something in her voice put Gina on alert. "Is everything okay? If you need help, tell me now."

"I don't! It's super busy, but I'm handling it," Carrie assured, sounding extra perky.

Too perky. Gina's worry radar kicked up again. But then, like herself, her assistant thrived on deadlines and stress, so maybe the bubbly enthusiasm was for real.

"Look for an updated report on the Grant stores tomorrow," Carrie added.

"Do you think you could send it this afternoon? With the funeral tomorrow, I doubt I'll be checking email until the following day."

"I'll try. How are you?"

Gina didn't have to think long about that. She'd just been kissed more thoroughly than she could ever remember, by a man she had no business kissing, and already she wanted more. She was a confused wreck.

She shook her head. "At the moment, I'm driving my uncle's old four-speed truck down an all-but-deserted two-lane highway to his attorney's office."

"That doesn't sound fun. You take care of yourself and your family, and don't worry about me or work. Things are great here."

Gina disconnected, dismissed her concerns and went right back to thinking of Zach's kisses.

## Chapter Four

Thanks to the meeting with the attorney, checking her email—and not finding the report from Carrie—and running some errands, Gina didn't return to the ranch until nearly dinnertime. She walked in the back door with her arms full. Her family was in the kitchen—Sophie and Redd getting out cutlery and dinner plates and Gloria putting one of the casseroles into the oven.

"You're finally back." Gloria lifted her cheek for a kiss. "What took so long?"

"Honestly, Glo." Sophie tsked. "Give the girl a chance to catch her breath."

"For goodness' sake, Sophie. It's a figure of speech, not a criticism."

Gina ignored the petty squabbling and set down her things. "I met with Matt Granger. Then I ran around, doing all the things he needed me to do. I also checked my email and stopped off at Spenser's to buy trash bags and boxes for when I sort through Uncle Lucky's things. Since you're all here…"

She leaned against the counter and crossed her arms. "You all knew Uncle Lucky left the ranch to me instead of Uncle Redd. Why didn't one of you say something?"

Her uncle and cousins exchanged looks. "We thought it might be better coming from someone else. I need a kiss, too," Sophie said, as if their keeping a secret from Gina was no big deal.

Obligingly, she kissed her cousin's wizened cheek.

"Were you surprised when Matt told you?" Uncle Redd asked, offering his cheek, too.

Gina kissed him, then straightened and frowned. "I would've been if Zach hadn't warned me."

"*Zach* told you?" Gloria's eyebrows shot up. "I didn't expect that."

"I'm thankful he did," Gina said. "I don't like surprises like that."

Sophie looked contrite. "We were afraid you'd be upset."

"That doesn't mean you should avoid the subject. How would you feel if I did that to you?"

Her uncle gave her a sheepish look.

"I guess we should have told you," Gloria said.

Sophie bit her lip. "Please don't be angry with us."

She looked so anxious that Gina kissed her cheek again. "I'll live. But from now on, please don't keep secrets from me."

"Understood." Uncle Redd eyed the folders she'd set on the counter. "What's all that?"

"Papers I took to the attorney. I'm going to put them away and drop these trash bags and boxes in Uncle Lucky's office. I'll be back."

In the office, Gina removed the painting and opened Uncle Lucky's safe. She returned the folders and then searched for the packet the attorney had described. She found what she was looking for in the back corner of the safe.

She didn't have to fold back the layers of tissue paper to know what was inside—the watch Uncle Lucky had inherited from his father, who'd gotten it from *his* father. According to the attorney, for some time now, Uncle Lucky had thought of Zach as the son he'd never had and had asked that the watch be passed on to him. Gina knew that Zach would be touched.

Over his seventy-four years, Uncle Lucky had known his share of ranch hands. As far as she knew, he'd never grown as close to any of the others as he had to Zach. It was comforting to know that someone her uncle cared about had lived on the ranch these past few years.

She should've been here, too. Once again, her guilt stirred. Every year, Andersen, Coats and Mueller closed from December 24th through January 1st, and she could easily have flown home last year. Her uncles and cousins would have loved that.

Instead, she'd spent Christmas Eve at a party with Wayne. That night, he'd stayed over, but early the next morning, he'd left for a family get-together, and she'd gone to Lise's townhouse for brunch. She'd spent the rest of the day alone, filling the time with work.

This Christmas was bound to be even more lonely, but she wasn't about to come back here in a month.

She locked up the safe, placing the package in her purse.

When she returned to the kitchen, mouthwatering smells greeted her. Her stomach growled, demanding to be fed. Someone had set the table, and the family was seated around it. "That smells so good, and I am so hungry," she said, licking her lips.

"The casserole needs to bake at least another thirty minutes, so I'm afraid dinner won't be for a little while yet, but sit down and relax." Gloria patted the chair next to her. "Tell us what else Matt Granger had to say."

"You all know that Uncle Lucky wasn't exactly flush

with cash. There's enough money in the bank to pay salaries and the bills for a few months but not much extra."

The next part was difficult, but Gina needed to say it. She cleared her throat. "Mr. Granger explained that even though Uncle Lucky left the ranch to me, I'm not legally bound to keep it. He said that what I do with the ranch is up to me."

"What do you plan to do?" Uncle Redd asked, but his resigned expression told her he already knew the answer.

"This is what I told Zach and Mr. Granger." Gina made sure to look each of her relatives in the eye. "I've had some wonderful times here, but I can't keep the ranch. I guess I'll put it on the market, hopefully before I leave town."

In the beat of silence that filled the room, Gina's family traded looks.

Sophie shook her head. "I'm afraid that won't work. You see, next Thursday is Thanksgiving, and Carole Plett always closes her real-estate office for the entire week."

"Then I'll talk to her tomorrow. She'll be at the funeral, right?"

"Unfortunately, she won't," Gloria said. "I was at Anita's Cut and Curl this morning, getting my hair done for tomorrow. Carole happened to be there, too. Her daughter in Elk Ridge just had a little girl, Carole's first grandchild. As you can imagine, she's eager to get her hands on that baby, and since the real-estate business is slow this time of year, she decided to close up shop this afternoon. She's probably pulling into Elk Ridge just about now."

"That reminds me," Uncle Redd said. "We got a sympathy card from her today. She donated a big bouquet of flowers for the funeral."

"That was real sweet of her." Sophie looked pleased. "I was over at the church earlier today, making sure everything is ready, and those flowers look just beautiful."

So much for listing the property while she was in town. Gina sighed. "I guess I'll call her from Chicago."

"That's a real good idea, honey," Uncle Redd said. "It'll give you more time to think about whether you really want to sell."

"I don't have to think, I—"

Uncle Redd fixed Gina with a stern look she rarely saw, and the rest of her words died in her throat. "This land has been in our family for generations," he said. "It ought to stay in our family."

"He's right, cookie," Sophie said. "You should pass it on to your children—when you have them."

Gloria narrowed her eyes. "Speaking of children, how much longer are you going to wait before you get married and start a family?"

Gina gave her a wry look. "Gee, Gloria, why don't you ask me something *really* personal?"

Undaunted, her cousin settled her hand on her ample hips. "I'm family. I can ask you anything I please. And don't try to put me off."

"Fine. At the moment I'm not dating—I just don't have time. You know how busy I am with work."

"What happened to Wayne?" Sophie asked. "He sounded like a nice fella."

"He is," Gina said. "But things didn't work out."

Hating the pitying looks on her cousins' faces, she added, "It wasn't a bad breakup or anything. We realized we didn't love each other and that we didn't have a future together. We parted on good terms." She shrugged. "I promise you that someday I'll get married and start a family. But it won't be for a while."

"But you're thirty years old." Gloria frowned. "You should already be married and settled down. Why, when I was your age, I'd already been married and widowed."

Gloria's husband, Harvey, had died in Vietnam and she'd never recovered. As far as Gina knew, she hadn't dated since.

"Tony and I tried to have kids." Sophie gave her head a sorrowful shake. "But I kept losing them early in the second trimester."

"My first wife couldn't get pregnant at all," Uncle Redd said. "The second one said that taking care of me was enough and my third had had her tubes tied. If this family is to continue, it's up to you."

The constant pressure to marry and have babies never stopped. "Hey, this is the twenty-first century. I'm still young and I have a career, remember? I love what I do, and I'm darn good at it. That's why I was promoted to the assistant vice-president position last spring."

"And we're all real proud of you," Uncle Redd said. Sophie and Gloria nodded enthusiastically. "But couldn't you hold on to the ranch?"

Gina hated to disappoint her family, but they needed to understand. "Who's going to pay the ranch crew's salaries when the money runs out? Even if I paid them with my own funds, and I'm not going to do that, we all know that sooner or later, the ranch will need even more cash to stay afloat."

She wasn't about to confess that despite her large paycheck, keeping the creditors off her back kept her virtually broke. She was too humiliated. "Besides, I live more than eleven hundred miles away," she went on. "How could I possibly run the ranch? And don't tell me I should move back here. I have a good job in Chicago, and I like living there."

A stony silence met her words.

"Times are tough," Uncle Redd said. "There's no guarantee you'll be able to sell the Lucky A."

Gina hoped he was wrong. "Well, then—"

A knock at the door cut her off. Relieved at the interruption and wondering who had come to pay their respects, she jumped up. "I'll get that."

She opened the door and found Zach.

"HEY," ZACH SAID, wiping his feet on the mat.

"Hi." Gina looked surprised to see him—and a little confused. "I didn't expect to see you tonight."

"Your cousins invited me to dinner."

"And you're right on time, Zach," Gloria called out from the kitchen. "Don't just stand there heating up the great outdoors, Gina. Let the man in."

Gina stepped back. Her cheeks were flushed, reminding him of how she looked after he'd kissed her a few hours ago. Not that he needed reminding. He'd thought of little else since.

"You're just in time, Zach—the casserole will be ready in a few minutes," Gloria said. "If you haven't washed up, now's the time."

No one moved except Gina. Walking beside her toward the utility room, he smelled her perfume and the subtle scent of woman underneath. And wanted to taste her again. Just what he needed.

He stood back while she washed her hands at the big utility room sink. "You okay with me being here tonight?" he asked over the hiss of water.

"As long as you don't try to convince me to change my mind about the Lucky A."

He glanced at her sexy mouth. "I can't guarantee that."

Her eyes darkened. She quickly rinsed and dried her hands. She seemed flustered.

"Speaking of the ranch, how was the meeting with the attorney?" he asked as he lathered up.

"Thanks to you, I didn't get any surprises. I can't believe my family didn't say anything. I told them that I'm going to sell."

Zach turned off the tap and took the towel from Gina. "I'll bet that went over big."

"Not so much. I'm tired of thinking about what I should and shouldn't do with the ranch. Could we please change the subject?"

If she was still thinking about it, then she hadn't made up her mind after all. Zach smiled to himself. "Sure."

"Did you know that Uncle Lucky left you a few things?"

"Me?" He couldn't imagine what, but he was intrigued.

She nodded. "I'll tell you about it after dinner."

He could live with that.

They returned to the kitchen. Zach couldn't help noting the sly looks on the faces of Gina's family. What were they up to?

"Zach, you'll sit next to Gina," Sophie directed a little too offhandedly.

So that was the game. They wanted to push him and Gina together. Gina closed her eyes for a moment and sighed.

Zach sat down to a bubbling casserole and thick slabs of homemade bread.

When everyone had filled their plate, Gloria smiled at him. "How was your day?"

"Busy." He told them about the broken heater in the big water tank.

"What happened there?" Sophie asked, pointing to the cut on the underside of his forearm.

"I got into a little argument with a barbed wire fence."

"Ow."

Zach had suffered worse. "It'll heal."

His plate was empty, but he was still hungry.

Gloria noticed. "Please, have more. You wouldn't believe how many casseroles we have to eat up."

He helped himself and dug in.

"Uncle Lucky left some of his things to Zach," Gina said near the end of the meal.

"Oh?" Sophie looked as intrigued as Zach.

Gloria and Redd leaned forward eagerly. "What did he leave you, Zach?"

"Gina hasn't said yet."

"Spit it out, girl," Redd ordered. "Before we all die of curiosity."

"I was going to wait until after the meal, but all right." Gina turned to Zach. "Uncle Lucky left you his horse, Lightning."

"Ah." Redd sat back with an approving nod. "Lucky loved that horse so. It's fitting that he'd want you to have her."

The horse was a beauty and as fast as her name. Zach was deeply moved. "I never expected that."

"There's more," Gina said. "You also get his saddle."

The handcrafted saddle had been one of Lucky's prized possessions. "Are you sure?" Zach asked.

Gina nodded. "He put it in his will."

"I remember when Lucky bought that," Sophie said. "It was the year all of us took Gina to the state fair in Great Falls." She smiled fondly at Gina. "You were about ten."

"I remember that! I was with Uncle Lucky when we stopped at the saddle maker's booth. He had a big, round belly that stretched his shirt so tight, I was sure all the buttons would pop off."

Her family chuckled. She had them all wrapped around her baby finger. Zach could see why. With her eyes sparkling and that pretty smile on her face, she could charm a barn rat.

"As I recall, your daddy also wanted a saddle." Redd shook his head.

Gina's smile faded. "I remember that, too. My parents had a big fight over it. Mom wouldn't let Dad spend the money. They didn't speak to each other for days after that."

Zach absorbed the information with interest. Except for Gina, the entire Arnett family seemed to have the frugal gene. But Gina earned enough to buy whatever she wanted.

The family looked solemn now, their thoughts on that day long ago.

"I'm honored to have that saddle," Zach said. "I'll take good care of it. Every time I use it and whenever I ride Lightning, I'll think of Lucky."

Redd nodded. "Now that's real nice. I know that wherever Lucky is right now, he's grinning like a son of a— Like a fool."

"He left you one more thing," Gina said. "I put it in my purse in the other room." She went to get it.

Lucky had already given him more than enough. Zach frowned.

When Gina returned, she handed him a tissue-wrapped package. "This is for you."

Zach had no idea what it could be.

"Is that what I think it is?" Gloria asked, her hand over her heart.

He carefully unwrapped the package. A moment later, he held up a gold pocket watch that looked well used.

Redd nodded. "That watch belonged to our grandfather and then to my daddy."

"Then it should be yours," Zach said.

"Lucky was the oldest son, so it went to him. I got Granddaddy's gold cufflinks. Lucky wore that watch for special occasions. You'll need to wind it to make it run, but it still keeps perfect time. Next to that saddle, it was his most prized possession. He was supposed to pass it to his son. You were the son he never had, Zach, and it's good that he wanted you to have it."

Over the years Zach had received his share of expensive presents, but no one had ever given him such a meaningful gift. He swallowed thickly. "I will cherish this watch forever."

Gina and her cousins teared up, and Redd cleared his throat and wiped his eyes. "You're a fine young man, Zach Horton."

He hadn't always been. Without Lucky, he might still be lost. Dearly missing his friend, Zach curled his fingers around the watch.

"You'll need to get yourself a chain for it, Zach," Redd said. "Put it in your pocket for now so you don't lose it."

"I wouldn't want to break it."

"You won't."

Zach slipped the watch into his hip pocket. In the trailer where he lived there wasn't a place to display it, but he intended to find one.

Gina stood to clear the table and rinse the dishes, and Zach loaded them into Lucky's portable dishwasher.

"Who wants coffee?" Sophie asked.

"Coffee?" The expression on Gina's face was priceless. He couldn't stem his laughter, and she laughed, too.

Sophie frowned. "What's so funny?"

"I made a pot of Uncle Lucky's coffee this morning," Gina said. "Zach knows how terrible it was—he had a cup."

As soon as Gloria heard that Zach had been here that

morning, she smiled. Sophie looked pleased, and Redd looked like the Cheshire cat.

They weren't exactly subtle.

"I promise you that this coffee will taste much better," Sophie said. "I brought over a different kind and I scoured Lucky's coffeepot from top to bottom. I don't think the poor thing has been cleaned in a decade."

"I never even thought of that. Okay, I'll give it a try." Zach shrugged. "If you're game, so am I."

"I'll get some of those chocolate-chip cookies Mrs. Yancy dropped off yesterday," Gloria said. "They're delicious."

"Shouldn't we save them in case someone stops by?" Gina asked.

"We won't have any guests tonight. They're all waiting for the funeral tomorrow."

In no time, Zach and the Arnetts were enjoying cookies and decent-tasting coffee.

"You're right—this is good," Gina said. "I think I'll have a second cup. Anyone else?"

Zach and the others shook their heads.

"Careful or you'll be up till all hours," Redd warned.

"That's okay. I have work to do."

"Why don't you take the night off, cookie?" Sophie patted her hand. "You look so worn out."

"I am pretty tired." Gina said, massaging the space between her brows.

"You need rest so that you can be strong tomorrow."

"You're right. Forget that second cup of coffee. I'll go to bed early."

An image of Gina in bed filled Zach's mind. He pictured her in a black satin teddy that revealed all her curves. He imagined slowly peeling the garment off her body and making her forget all about sleeping…

He caught himself and shut down his thoughts. Lucky had just died. Gina was grieving, and so was Zach. He shouldn't be thinking about sex.

What kind of man was he, lusting over Lucky's niece when he was supposed to be focused on convincing her to keep the ranch?

She wasn't even his type. He steered clear of women like her. Steered clear of getting involved, period. Getting involved meant questions, and he wasn't about to explain his past to Gina or anyone else.

They were arguments he'd repeated to himself several times today. That didn't stop him from fantasizing about her.

"You're frowning, Zach." Sophie looked concerned. "I thought you liked Mrs. Yancy's cookies."

"They're great." Forcing a bland expression, he helped himself to a few more. "I was thinking about the funeral."

Gloria let out a weighty sigh. "It's on all our minds."

"What time is the service?" Gina asked.

"Ten-thirty." Redd stacked his mug on his empty dessert plate. "But we don't know how long it'll last—that will depend on how many people share stories about Lucky."

Zach expected to hear a whole lot of those. Most everyone had counted the rancher as a friend.

"As soon as the service ends, there will be a reception in the church's rec room," Gloria said. "Then the five of us will come back here and scatter Lucky's ashes."

Gina gave a solemn nod.

Nothing about it sounded easy. Tomorrow was guaranteed to be a long and difficult day.

## Chapter Five

On the day of the funeral, Gina woke up feeling sad and heavy. It was early and still dark outside, and she flipped on the bedside-table lamp. Before she even got out of bed, she checked her phone. There were no messages.

She speed-dialed Carrie's cell phone. The assistant didn't pick up. Instead of leaving a message, Gina hung up and called the main office line. "Good morning, Marsha. Will you put me through to Carrie?"

"Of course, but you'll get her voice mail. I haven't seen her yet this morning."

It was almost nine in Chicago. "That's two days in a row," Gina muttered. On this of all days, her assistant was the last person she needed to worry about.

"I wish I knew where she was," Marsha said, and Gina pictured the forty-something secretary giving her head a disapproving shake. "Is there something I can do to help?"

"If you're not too busy. She was supposed to email me a report yesterday, with updates on the various campaigns for each of my clients, but I didn't receive it. I won't have access to email today, but if you can find the report, I'd love to know what the numbers are."

"Let me put you on hold and see what I can find."

While Gina waited, she opened the closet and pulled out the outfit she'd packed for the funeral. At the time, the black suit and gray blouse had seemed appropriate. But now that Zach had suggested using humor, she wished she'd brought something less somber.

On a whim, she plucked a green holly-sprig pin with red berries from the jewelry she'd tossed into her carry-on. The holiday season didn't officially start for another week, but she didn't think anyone would mind.

"You'll never guess what I found in Carrie's office—Carrie herself," Marsha said when she returned to the phone. "She was asleep at her desk. Apparently she worked late last night and dropped off. She was pretty upset when I woke her and she realized what had happened. She's going home to shower and change clothes, and she asked if she could call you with the numbers later."

"Poor Carrie." Gina felt bad for her assistant. She thought about asking one of her colleagues to step in and take some of the load off Carrie's shoulders, but she didn't have time to explain and review the details just now. "Just make sure she emails that report sometime today, and ask her to call me this afternoon. I should be able to talk by four Montana time at the latest."

"I'll be thinking of you. There is one more thing you should know. Some of your clients called yesterday, and I'm not sure Carrie returned their calls."

Andersen, Coats and Mueller had built their reputation on quality service and excellent results, which meant seeing to the client's every need—which included returning calls promptly.

Growing more concerned by the minute, Gina frowned. "Would you email me the messages? Then please call and let the clients know where I am, and tell them that I'll contact them first thing on Monday morning."

Her stomach in knots, she disconnected. If her assistant flaked out on her, they were both in a world of trouble.

But she couldn't worry about any of that right now. Setting her work troubles aside, she turned her focus on the day ahead.

AS FUNERALS WENT, Lucky's wasn't half bad, Zach mused as he piloted Redd's station wagon and the Arnett family back to the ranch. Redd's was the only car big enough to seat five adults. The ranch crew followed behind the wagon, a melancholy contingent of cars and trucks that would leave Zach and the family to scatter the ashes on their own. The afternoon was overcast and cold, and Zach figured they were in for another snowstorm. He hoped it held off until the family dispersed Lucky's ashes.

It had been an emotionally draining day. Sophie and Gloria slumped on the bench seat up front, and in the back, Redd and Gina stared out their respective windows.

Zach patted Lucky's watch, which was attached to his pants by the chain he'd found at a jewelry store in the next town. Wearing the watch somehow helped. He glanced in the rearview mirror. As if Gina felt his stare, she turned from the window and solemnly met his gaze. Her eyes were red and swollen. Tears had washed away her makeup and her lipstick had worn off long ago, but she didn't need cosmetics to look pretty. She was what Lucky would have called a natural beauty.

"How're you doing?" he asked softly.

She squared her shoulders. "I'm okay."

As he drove down the highway toward the ranch, he thought about her funny yet poignant eulogy. She'd touched him and everyone else, and sniffling sounds had filled the little church.

She'd dressed for the occasion in a black pantsuit with a

festive pop of color on the lapel and high, black heels that made him wish she were wearing a skirt so that he could look at her legs. His grief didn't stop him from wanting her, and apparently he wasn't the only one. More than one male in attendance had checked her out.

"I just thought of something," Gloria said as they neared the ranch. "At least three inches of snow are on the ground and the earth is frozen solid. How are we supposed to scatter Lucky's ashes?"

Sophie's fingers worried the straps of her purse. "Maybe we should hold on to them until the spring thaw."

"Months from now?" Redd snorted. "By then, Gina might have sold the ranch."

Sophie and Gloria swiveled their heads around to eye her.

With her lip firmly between her teeth, she dug in her purse for a tissue, setting off a flurry of tears and nose blowing.

Zach cleared his throat. "Lucky loved the river. We could scatter the ashes there."

"But it's frozen," Gloria said.

"Not at its deepest points. We'll find a place where it isn't." Zach turned up the gravel driveway, passing under the Lucky A Ranch sign that hung under an iron arch spanning the entrance. As he turned toward the house, the caravan of vehicles behind them blinked their lights and headed for their respective trailers.

"Save your good shoes and take my car over to your trailer, Zach," Redd said as Zach pulled up close to the back door. "Get changed and we'll see you back here shortly."

Zach nodded and escorted Gloria and Sophie to the door.

When he returned to the house, he left the engine running, headed up the steps and knocked on the door.

They were all waiting for him. Gina had changed into jeans, winter boots and a body-hugging pullover sweater the color of whipped butter.

After everyone was in the car and buckled up, he headed slowly toward the river. "The ground is good and hard. I should be able to drive almost to the riverbank."

The ranch hands had offered to do all the afternoon chores, giving him the rest of the day off. In the distance, cattle huddled together around fresh feed the crew had just delivered. Snow flurries swirled through the air. If they wanted to beat the harder stuff, they'd best get moving.

A scant few yards from the water, Zach pulled to a stop. The wind had kicked up and the icy air stung his face.

He took hold of Sophie and Gloria. Gina grasped Redd's arm. She'd traded her expensive coat for a burgundy-colored down jacket and scarf and a stylish hat that protected her ears.

Standing at the riverbank, she frowned. "The entire river looks frozen to me."

"Not out there." Zach pointed to a dark patch of water at the widest part of the river, a few yards away.

"But that's halfway across. It can't be safe."

He nodded. "Trust me, the ice is thick. It'll hold us."

"All five of us? Are you sure?"

"If I weren't, I wouldn't have suggested bringing the ashes out here. I wouldn't put you or anyone else at risk."

Gina shot a worried glance at her cousins and Redd. "Maybe they should watch from here."

"That seems wise," Redd said. "It isn't that I don't trust your judgment, Zach. But at our ages, we can't risk slipping and falling."

"That's right." Gloria moved closer to Redd and Sophie. "We'll say our goodbyes from here. What about you, Gina?"

"I want to do this." Gina turned her impossibly big eyes on Zach. "You'll come with me?"

A snowflake clung to her eyelashes. He had the urge to kiss it away, but instead he nodded and took the urn from her.

She hooked her hand through his arm, and he swore he felt her warmth through her fur-lined glove. They made their way cautiously across the ice. Less than a foot away from the sluggish water that was on the verge of freezing, he pulled her to a stop. "We'd best not go any closer."

Gina nodded and, with her teeth, tugged off her gloves. She shoved them into her pockets and took the urn from Zach. She opened it and held it up. "Goodbye, Uncle Lucky. Be at peace," she said over the wind.

Beautiful words that would've meant more if she was keeping the ranch. Zach silently pledged to continue trying to convince her.

From the riverbank, Gloria and Sophie called out their own final messages, and Redd added, "God speed."

"Goodbye, friend," Zach murmured, his chest tight with feeling.

He and Gina shared a long look filled with mutual loss and grief. Then with a thrust of her arms, she sent Lucky's ashes flying. They mingled briefly with the snow before dropping quietly into the water.

Silent and solemn, she handed the empty urn to Zach. Her hands were red, and she tugged on her gloves with clumsy fingers. He knew how cold they were. His own face was numb, and he regretted leaving his woolen ski mask at the trailer.

Gina hooked her arm through his again and they made their way toward the bank. Snow was coming down hard now, and the sky had grown steadily darker. Zach guessed it was after four. Gloria, Sophie and Redd headed for the car and piled into the backseat.

"At least one of you should ride in the front with Zach and me," she said as Zach opened the passenger door.

"We don't mind sitting back here together." Redd winked.

It was clear that they wanted Zach and Gina to get together.

Now, there was a match doomed before it even started.

Regardless, today they'd shared something neither of them would ever forget.

As soon as the engine purred to life, Zach turned the heat on full blast.

"That feels good." Gina held her hands in front of the vent.

She practically hugged the door. Even so, Zach was as keenly attuned to her presence as if she was sitting close.

She pulled off her hat and he caught a whiff of her flowery perfume. His body stirred. This was getting old.

"I don't feel the heat yet." Gloria stomped her feet and rubbed her hands together. "It's beastly cold. I wouldn't be surprised if we all had frostbite."

"The way we're all bundled up?" Sophie harrumphed. "You're so melodramatic, Glo. You should've gone into acting."

At the house, Gina exited while Zach helped her cousins.

The empty evening stretched before him, as gray as the sky. He wanted to join the family, but he'd been with them all day and didn't want to intrude any further. "I'll leave you to it," he said, shoving his hands into the pockets of his parka.

"Leave us to what?" Sophie's lips quirked.

He shrugged. "You probably want time alone, with just the family."

"Nonsense," Redd said. "You're as much a part of the family as the rest of us. But I happen to have an ulterior motive—I was hoping you could whip up some hot toddies to help us get warm. I'm still thinking about the ones you made last year during that stretch of subzero weather. Best I ever tasted."

Gloria grasped Zach's arm. "You heard the man. Please stay."

"All right." Zach held the door for everyone.

Inside, Gina studied him with a thoughtful expression. "Hot toddies aren't exactly the kind of thing people our age drink," she said. "Where did you learn to make them?"

"In a different life." An easy life of wealth and luxury Zach had once taken for granted. Life at the Lucky A was harder and leaner, but in the three years since he'd sold his company and taken a job here, he didn't miss much of what he'd given up. He was certainly happier.

"Did you own a bar or something?" Gina asked while her cousins dug out the ingredients for the drink.

"In a manner of speaking." He hung up his coat. "When you were fourteen, Lucky taught you to drive. When I was that age, my father taught me to mix drinks. He thought that if I played bartender during the parties he liked to throw, I'd be too busy to get into trouble."

"Did it work?"

"Let's just say, I learned to sneak my drinks when no one was looking. It was a great gig—until I got caught."

Sophie tsked, Gloria covered a smile with her hand and Redd grinned and said, "I'll bet your daddy whupped you good."

Looking amused, Gina arched her eyebrows. Her

cheeks were pink from the cold, and for the first time all day, her eyes were bright and filled with humor.

"I got a stern lecture, which was probably worse than any spanking," Zach replied with a deadpan expression.

As he'd hoped, they all laughed. He joined in. After the weighty day, laughing felt good.

As soon as Gina hung up her coat and tugged off her boots, she moved toward the stairs. "I'm going to make a few calls. I'll be down in a little while."

Zach shook his head. She couldn't even take the full day off for her uncle's funeral—a needed reminder that he wasn't interested.

"DAMN YOU, CARRIE," Gina muttered as she sat on the bed and checked her phone messages.

Out of respect for her family and the funeral, she'd left her phone in her room today. At some point this afternoon, Carrie had called with an update and numbers. Unfortunately, she'd repeated the same information she'd already shared. And she didn't mention the client calls she'd failed to return.

She was exhausted, but Gina also suspected that despite Carrie's assurances that she could handle the temporary responsibilities she was saddled with, she wasn't ready.

Gina thought about telling Kevin, but she wasn't ready just yet. She definitely needed to ask one of her colleagues for help. As busy as they all were, they wouldn't appreciate having to take on more work. Carrie wouldn't like it, either, but she obviously couldn't handle the workload by herself.

Marsha had also called with the names and numbers from the past two days' calls and let Gina know she'd contacted them.

Outside, darkness had fallen. Gina checked her watch. The funeral, reception and spreading the ashes had taken longer than she'd imagined. In Chicago it was after five and the Friday before Thanksgiving to boot. The office was already gearing down for the holiday and upcoming short workweek, and Gina doubted that anyone would be there now. All the same, she left a message for Carrie.

She also tried Carrie's cell, but her assistant didn't pick up. Well, she had that dinner date tonight. Gina left a message that ended with, "First thing Monday morning, you and I need to talk. Expect my call at nine a.m. Chicago time."

Having done all that she could for now, she stood. She caught a glimpse of herself in the mirror. Somehow, her makeup had disappeared, and she looked all washed out. If only she'd realized sooner. Wanting to look better for her family, and yes, for Zach, she freshened up her makeup and ran a comb through her hair. There.

She looked better, but between the funeral and worrying about Carrie, she felt as if she'd been through the wringer.

Needing the comfort of her family and Zach, she headed downstairs to rejoin them.

## Chapter Six

A roaring fire crackled in the fireplace, as if this were a normal November evening at the Lucky A. It wasn't. Uncle Lucky had been a huge presence in Gina's life, and his passing left a big hole in her heart. That he wasn't here to tease her and make her laugh put a definite damper on things, but Zach and her family were good company.

Having consumed one of his delicious hot toddies before dinner and two glasses of wine with the meal, she was finally relaxed. Zach and Uncle Redd had brought up a set of old TV trays from the basement and they'd eaten in front of the fire, polishing off a whole casserole, most of a chocolate cake and two bottles of wine—with numerous toasts to Uncle Lucky.

Uncle Redd set down his cake plate and patted his belly. "That was real tasty," he said, stretching and yawning. "It's been a long day, and I'm ready to go home." He gestured at Sophie and Gloria. "Get your coats, girls."

Too full and comfortable to move just yet, Gina scrutinized her uncle from her chair. "It's stopped snowing, but there are at least a few more inches on the ground. The roads are sure to be slippery, and you've had quite a bit to drink. Plus it's dark. Why don't you stay here? There's room for all of you."

Uncle Redd shook his head. "We'll do that at Christmas. I can't leave the dogs alone overnight. I'm not driving more than a few miles and I could do it blindfolded, so the dark isn't a problem. Besides, I only had the one hot toddy and half a glass of wine, and you saw how much food I put away tonight. I'm as sober as I was when I got up this morning."

He shot a wry look at Sophie and Gloria, who'd helped Gina and Zach drink the wine. "I can't speak for your cousins, though."

The women glanced at each other and giggled. Slightly drunk herself, Gina smiled.

In no time, everyone was in the kitchen, Gina and Zach helping the older ones into their coats.

After all they'd been through today, Gina felt very close to her family. She hated to see them go and dreaded spending the night alone in the house. But she wasn't going to admit it.

"Will I see you tomorrow?" she asked after she hugged and kissed each of them.

Gloria shook her head. "Probably not, honey. Saturday is the day Sophie and I do our house cleaning. Besides, you'll be sorting through Lucky's papers and things, and we'd probably just get in the way. Why don't you come to our house Sunday night for dinner? We'll plan our Thanksgiving meal." She smiled at Zach. "It goes without saying that you're invited again this year—both for Thanksgiving and Christmas."

"I appreciate that," Zach said. "Count me in."

Without Uncle Lucky, both holiday celebrations were bound to feel dreary. Gina half wished she could come back at Christmas.

Redd opened the door to leave. "Don't stay up late, you two." Winking, he closed it behind them.

"They couldn't be more obvious about pushing us together." Gina shook her head in disbelief. "I love them all dearly, but sometimes—make that a lot of the time—they drive me crazy."

"They aren't so bad."

"That's because they're on their best behavior when you're around. You should hear them nag and question me about when I'm going to get married. They're worried that if I don't get married and have kids soon, the Arnett family line will die out."

"What do you tell them?"

"That I'm barely thirty and I have plenty of time. I'm not even dating right now."

"Too busy working?"

"That, and I'm also picky."

"Let me guess, you're looking for a CEO to come along and sweep you off your feet."

She laughed. "He doesn't have to be a CEO as long as he's ambitious. My family doesn't understand at all."

Zach was silent and his expression was unreadable. Gina wished she knew what he was thinking. "Men don't have the same kind of pressure as women," she added.

"Sure we do, but in different ways. You have a choice of whether or not to make your name in the world. We don't have that choice."

"Your family puts that kind of pressure on you?"

"Every man's does."

"And you're rebelling."

For a moment he looked puzzled. Then his eyes narrowed a fraction. "You mean because I'm a ranch foreman. You're a white-collar snob." He snorted and headed back to the living room.

She was offended. "I am not! I just… You're really smart, Zach. What you said about Uncle Lucky at the funeral today was eloquent and moving. You have all this potential, and…" By his grim expression, she saw that she'd only made things worse, and she let the words trail off.

"You're wondering why I don't do what you do? Put in eighty-hour workweeks chasing after the next deal? That's an empty life I don't choose to live."

None too gently, he began to stack the dessert plates.

She'd really hit a sore spot. "You're going to break something, Zach."

He set down the dishes and slapped the folding TV tables shut. "I'll take these back to the basement."

"I can do that later."

Tight-lipped, he hefted the five folded tables and strode toward the kitchen.

Those tables were heavy, yet he toted them as if they weighed nothing. Gina followed him, jogging to keep up. In the kitchen, she shot around him to open the basement door and flip on the lights down there.

His footsteps thudded down the wooden steps, each one sounding like a scold. Feeling terrible for insulting him, she chafed her arms.

Uncle Lucky's portable dishwasher was still hooked up to the kitchen faucet from after dinner. The cycle was finished, and she unhooked and wheeled it to its place against the wall.

She was about to put the clean dishes away when she heard Zach come up the stairs.

Her heart pounded. Twisting her hands at her waist, she met him at the top of the steps. He looked surprised. "What's wrong?"

"I just— Don't be angry, Zach."

"Damn straight, I'm mad. I don't like being judged, especially when you know nothing about me."

She was wearing flat ankle boots tonight, which gave

him a height advantage of at least four inches. Looming over her with a dark expression, he was intimidating, but she met his gaze. "Not for lack of asking. You won't tell me anything."

"My past is my business. It's over and done with, and I don't talk about it." He crossed his arms as if daring her to say one more word about the subject.

Frustrated, she offered something of an apology. "I won't bring up your past again, all right? But don't blame me for making assumptions. They're all I have to go on."

That didn't make him any happier, and she threw up her hands. "You should probably just go home," she said, hating the thought of his leaving like this, of being alone for the rest of the evening.

"I'll stay until the dishes are done. You empty the dishwasher and I'll bring in the stuff from the living room."

"That'd be nice. Thank you."

NOT IN THE best of moods, Zach turned and headed back to the living room. Of all the nights to have words with Gina. He didn't want to argue with her or leave things unsettled. The second he'd caught sight of her in the airport baggage claim, he'd known they were as mismatched as a cowboy boot and an expensive pump.

The problem was that every time he saw her, he wanted her more.

He shouldn't have kissed her yesterday, but he wasn't sorry he had.

The plates clattered loudly as he stacked them. Then he remembered Gina's warning to be careful. He collected the utensils and glasses with more care and brought them to the kitchen.

Gina was putting away the clean silverware and acknowledged him with a curt nod.

Time for an apology. He set the dirty dishes in the sink and waited for her to look at him. Her wary expression tugged at something in his chest. "Look, I don't want to fight with you," he said.

"I'm so sorry for what I said—what I implied." She swallowed loudly, her eyes filled with remorse. "That was rude and completely uncalled for."

"It was, but I overreacted. We've both been through a lot, especially today, and feelings are raw."

"It isn't just losing Uncle Lucky." She bit her lip. "I'm worried about things at work."

"Ah." She kept reminding him that work was her main priority, and he kept forgetting. Unable to think of a decent reply, Zach shook his head. "I'll grab my coat and let you get back to it."

"Tonight I don't want to do anything remotely work related," she said. "I don't even want to think about my job, but I'm so stressed out that I can't help it. Carrie, my assistant, isn't doing what she promised. She's supposed to take up the slack and handle the accounts while I'm here. I've only been gone three days, and already she's fallen behind. My clients expect blue-ribbon service. I can't risk losing them because of her."

Zach understood. "Ask a colleague to step in and help."

"I'm going to have to," she said. "But everyone is trying to clear off their desks before Wednesday, when we close for the long Thanksgiving weekend."

"Have you talked to your boss?"

"Not yet." She sighed. "It's a bit of a mess. My assistant and I both assured him that she was up to the responsibility. He isn't exactly the compassionate type and I worry that he'll question my ability to manage. Even if I do find someone to step in, I'll have to take the time to explain what needs to be done. Which means I'll be stuck spending more time on work when I'd rather focus on the things I need to do here before I leave. Like sort through Uncle Lucky's papers and his personal effects and figure out what to keep and what I can toss. How am I supposed to get it all done?"

"Winter is a slow time for ranchers. I'll do what I can. Other people have offered to help, too. We can't sort through Lucky's papers for you, but we can get rid of the newspapers and old magazines and clean out the basement. You just need to ask."

"Thanks. I'll sort everything out and let you know." She gave him a small smile. "Sorry for dumping on you like that."

"No problem." Zach felt for her. "I remember when my grandfather died. My family put what we didn't want or need immediately into storage. It was years before anyone looked through that stuff. You already have Lucky's financial papers. You could go through the rest of his things some other time."

That stubborn look crossed her face. "I don't want to put it off, Zach. I don't think Uncle Lucky would want me to." She pulled the last of the cutlery from the open dishwasher and put it away. "I feel bad enough that I didn't come home more often while he was alive. The least I can do is take the time and care to sort through his things now."

Her shoulders slumping, she fiddled with the knob on the silverware drawer and avoided his gaze. She was easy to read. Guilt was weighing her down.

Having been there himself, Zach knew how heavy that load was. He moved toward her. "Letting the guilt eat you alive won't do you or Lucky any good," he said. "Like he used to tell me, don't beat yourself up over things you can't change."

Her curious expression told him that she wondered what he'd beaten himself up about. But Lucky had been the last person to hear about that, and Zach was not going to revisit his sorry past ever again.

"My uncle gave you good advice, but I don't know that I can follow it."

"If I did, you can. You look like you could use a hug," he said, surprising himself.

He opened his arms, and she walked into them.

Without her heels, she barely reached his shoulder. As strong a woman as she was, her bones were fine and delicate. Zach tucked her against the hollow of his shoulder and rested his chin on the top of her head.

After a few moments, he felt the tension drain out of her, felt her relax. Perfume and the womanly scent underneath filled his senses. "That's much better."

Closing his eyes, he kissed her head. She wriggled closer, her softness teasing his body to life.

Now who was tense? Zach loosened his hold on her and started to back away.

"Don't go." Hanging on tight, she looked up at him, her green eyes round and pleading. "I need you tonight. Kiss me, Zach."

All day he'd wanted to do exactly that—and more. But wanting her was wrong for them both, and kissing her was dangerous.

He should walk away now, while he still could. But she laced her arms around his neck and pulled him down, and he was lost.

Her lips were sweet and eager. He slid his tongue inside her mouth and explored. He sat her on the cutting board top of the dishwasher and stood between her long legs.

One kiss blended into another, each one burning into him. His body went hard with desire. Wanting to taste more of her, he ran his lips down the column of her neck. She liked that, especially when he nibbled the place where her neck met her shoulder.

Mindful of the tiny gold hoops in her ears, he gently tugged her earlobe with his teeth. She liked that, too.

Hands on her hips, he scooted her forward and moved in closer. Big mistake.

She stiffened. "No, Zach."

What was he doing? He was supposed to convince Gina to keep the ranch, not fool around with her.

He straightened and stepped back. Gina hopped down from the dishwasher and tugged her sweater over her hips. The soft wool stretched tight across her breasts.

Zach swallowed. "It's time for me to go."

He grabbed his coat and let himself out.

UPSTAIRS, GINA STARED at herself in the bathroom mirror. With her slightly swollen lips and her flushed cheeks, she looked as if she'd been thoroughly kissed.

And she had been. Closing her eyes, she replayed the thrill of Zach's demanding mouth on hers and the way his strong arms had felt around her.

She'd enjoyed his kisses all too much, had wanted more. Which was exactly why she'd stopped him. She wasn't into casual sex, nor was she about to get involved with Zach—even if he was intelligent and not at all the hard cowboy she'd first thought. She wanted a man with the drive and ambition to be more than a ranch foreman.

None of that stopped her from thinking about him.

His father had taught him to mix drinks so that he could bartend at parties. That didn't sound blue-collar. Did Zach's parents have money? Had he attended college? Why had he left Houston, what had brought him to

Saddlers Prairie and why was he working as a foreman on Uncle Lucky's rundown ranch?

Gina was beyond curious, but Zach was so close-mouthed about his past that she doubted she'd ever learn the answers from him.

That wasn't going to stop her from trying to find out more. Surely someone in Saddlers Prairie could tell her what she wanted to know. She would ask around and see what she could find out.

## Chapter Seven

There was nothing quite like waking up gradually in bed on a Saturday morning. After rising before dawn pretty much seven days a week for months, lazing about felt luxurious.

Yawning and stretching, Gina let her thoughts wander. Naturally they homed in on Zach. Everything he'd done yesterday, from giving a eulogy at the funeral to spreading Uncle Lucky's ashes to spending the evening with her family, had been above and beyond and proved what a great guy he was.

But he was a rancher, and his life was tough. Gina wanted an easier life, with a regular paycheck, raises and bonuses.

Which meant that Zach wasn't the guy for her.

But the way he made her feel when he kissed her... She went warm and soft inside. She wanted more in spite of herself.

*No,* she firmly told herself and sat up.

It was time to get up and get to work on the house. She would start sorting through Uncle Lucky's things, beginning with the contents of his desk.

After showering and dressing, Gina headed downstairs. While her cinnamon bread toasted and the coffeemaker percolated, she turned on her phone.

To her relief, Carrie had texted, letting her know she'd emailed the report Gina wanted and that she would wait for Gina's call Monday morning.

"That's more like it," Gina murmured. She was relieved and decided that for now, she wouldn't bother any of her colleagues with the request to help her assistant.

As she loaded her breakfast dishes into the dishwasher, she couldn't help remembering the kisses she and Zach had shared right there last night. Unbidden heat flooded her, and she wanted him again.

Exasperated with herself, she turned her back on the dishwasher and considered making plans to go out tonight and do something to take her mind off Zach.

Saddlers Prairie didn't offer much of a nightlife, but she needed something to fill the evening. Not that she didn't have plenty to keep her busy right here. It would be nice to get out, though, even for a little while. She needed to write thank-you notes to those who sent cards and flowers, so she could drive over to Spenser's and pick up some nice note cards and some chocolate. Then she'd check out the TV guide and look for a movie. And, what the heck, she'd check her email today after all.

What a fabulous Saturday night she had planned.

Armed with trash bags and boxes, Gina started for Uncle Lucky's office.

She was halfway down the hall when her cell phone rang. She glanced at the screen and saw that Autumn Naylor was calling. Autumn was a year older than she was, but they'd attended the one-room Saddlers Prairie grade school together. Both had been dirt poor and they'd developed a friendship of sorts.

"Hey, Autumn," she said, smiling.

"Hi, Gina. That was a nice service yesterday."

"I thought so, too. We were all glad to see you and your family."

Autumn and Cody had an adorable little girl and four foster sons they were raising at Hope Ranch.

"I know this is last minute," Autumn said. "But Cody and the boys are seeing a movie in Red Deer tonight. April goes to bed at seven, and I have the whole evening to myself. I'm throwing a pizza party, no guys allowed. You know everyone who's coming, either from school or the funeral, and I'd love for you to come. That is, if you can spare the time. I know you have a lot on your plate."

Gina jumped at the invitation. "I'll be working on the house all day, but I'm free this evening. What should I bring?"

"Nothing, but since the Pizza Palace is on your way here, it'd be great if you picked up the pizzas for me. I'll call and put them under my name."

"Sure," Gina said.

"Great. See you tonight."

Pleased to have something fun to look forward to, Gina hummed as she sat down at the desk.

Having done a cursory search through the drawers the other day, she didn't expect to find anything worth keeping. They contained packages of never-used pens and pencils, paper clips and sticky notes—enough to last years. Her thrifty uncle had always preferred to buy his supplies in bulk. She would donate them to the school, she decided as she filled a box.

She made short work of all but the fat bottom drawer, which was crammed with ancient-looking folders containing old bills and statements dating back decades.

Who knew why her uncle saved all this stuff, or why he kept his current statements in the safe. Not that it wasn't entertaining to see what groceries had cost twenty-five years ago. Otherwise, it was worthless.

She was tossing the folders into a trash bag and thinking about taking a coffee break when a yellowed folder label caught her eyes. It read *Beau and Marie* in faded ink. Her parents.

Curious, she opened the folder, which was thick with papers. At first she wasn't at all sure what she was looking at, but seeing her parents' signatures here and there filled her with nostalgia. Her father's sense of humor and self-deprecating laugh had often lightened up the most difficult times, while her mother's canning and baking skills had kept their stomachs relatively filled. And despite working two jobs and preserving food, she'd somehow found the time to make many of Gina's clothes—outfits that often rivaled the store-bought items the other girls wore but sometimes fell far short.

Even after all these years, Gina still missed them—but not the hard life they'd endured.

At the bottom of the file she found papers that made her widen her eyes and suck in a breath. Bankruptcy papers.

The one on top noted that shortly after her birth, her parents had declared bankruptcy.

Stunned, she sat back in her chair. No one had ever told her about this. Not a whisper, even after both her parents had died.

Something else her family had kept from her. It had happened a long time ago, so what was the big secret?

Of course, bankruptcy wasn't good; Gina got that, but she was family. She deserved to know! Fuming, she set the folder aside, stood and stalked into the kitchen. Next time she saw her relatives, they were going to hear about this.

Over a cup of reheated morning coffee, she thought about her parents' bankruptcy some more. Knowing about it explained a lot. Her mother's constant worry about money and her tight hold on the family purse strings, and her father's grudging acceptance that his wife controlled the checkbook.

They'd had a legitimate reason for their money problems. Thanks to a recession and hard times, the farm-equipment business had all but failed. To supplement the family income, her dad had started an equipment-repair business, which had brought in some cash. Both her parents had put in long hours, leaving Gina to fend for herself at home.

Another unsettling part of the whole thing was that, despite her own large paychecks and fat year-end bonuses, she also struggled to make ends meet.

In that way, she wasn't so different from her parents.

That was upsetting. She wasn't like them. She wasn't! Too restless to sit still, she carried her coffee to the window and stared out at the snow-covered backyard and the rolling pastures beyond.

The snow turned everything into a winter wonderland. But nothing could hide the hard-scrabble life her uncle and parents had lived. Gina's life was much easier, and she had the condo, high-end car and closet filled with beautiful clothes and shoes to prove it. Yes, she struggled to pay the bills, but her bonus would help her catch up.

Skating so close to the financial edge was nerve-racking, something she didn't want to think about right now. She pushed the thought away and stared at the back pasture and the herd of cattle lumbering toward an old flatbed, where four men tossed heavy bales of hay onto the ground.

Was that Zach? He was too far away for Gina to be sure, but... No, that was him. As the tallest man, he stood out. Even in a bulky winter jacket, she recognized his long, muscular, jeans-clad legs.

From out of nowhere, a sigh escaped her. She was relieved that for the moment he was out of reach and glad she had plans away from the ranch that evening.

With any luck, she could avoid Zach for a while and rein in her unwanted feelings.

MAN, IT WAS cold. Standing in the north pasture, Zach stomped his numb feet and glanced at the wintry blue sky. It didn't look like snow, but in Montana, you never knew. Between the bitter cold and ice and the seasonal downtime at the ranch, Montana winters were a bitch.

Not that any of the ranch hands complained. They were glad for the work and used their free hours to spend time with their families and visit the friends they had little time for during the rest of the year. Next week, Pete, Bert and Chet would take off for the Thanksgiving holiday, while Zach and Curly had Christmas Eve and Christmas Day off.

When the truck bed stood empty, Zach whipped off his hat and wiped the sweat from his forehead with his coat sleeve. "That's it for today."

Chet and Pete whooped and made for the truck.

Curly Gomez, wryly nicknamed for his bald head, hung back. He and Zach had become friends of sorts and often spent their Saturday evenings hanging out together. They headed for the barn on foot.

"What's on the agenda tonight?" Curly asked, his breath puffing from his lips like smoke.

Anything that would take his mind off Gina. After a hard evening last night—*hard* being the operative word— Zach needed to keep his distance.

The wanting inside him just wouldn't quit. It had been

a while since he'd scratched that particular itch, and he figured it was time to change that. "I'm thinking we grab a pizza at the Pizza Palace, then drive up the highway to Sparky's." The bar just outside town was a good place to hook up with a willing woman.

Curly grinned. "Pizza, beer and ladies—I'm game. It's your turn to drive."

Zach nodded. "I'll give you a call when I'm ready to go."

THE PIZZA PALACE was busy, but then it was a wintry Saturday night in Saddlers Prairie. Zach and Curly were in a booth and about to dig into their extra-large pizza when Curly leaned across the table toward him.

"Don't look now," he said under his breath, "but the dark-haired woman at the table to your left is checking you out."

"Yeah?" Zach took a big bite out of his pizza and surreptitiously glanced around. The woman was about his age, with long hair, full lips and big breasts—just his type. She gave him a friendly smile.

Oddly, aside from a spark of attraction, he didn't feel much interest. Unsmiling, he nodded at her and returned his focus to his dinner.

"What'd I tell you?" Curly said with a go-get-her smile.

"She's okay."

His friend's jaw dropped. "If you don't think she's hot, you need glasses."

She was hot enough. Unfortunately, Gina was the woman Zach wanted.

Frowning, he reached for a second slice and glanced at the door as it opened. Gina walked in.

Of all people. A certain part of his body woke up. He swore under his breath.

Curly glanced over his shoulder. "That's Gina."

"Yep."

"She's a real class act. I wonder what she's doing here?"

"She must want a Palace pizza."

"Well, it is one of the finest pizza joints around." Curly's mouth quirked. "The *only* pizza joint around."

She'd spotted him. Zach nodded. Looking a little uncomfortable, Gina headed uncertainly toward the table.

"Hello, Curly," she said, wearing a bright smile that faded when she turned her gazed to Zach. "Hi."

They shared a long look fraught with meaning. They hadn't seen each other since last night. In the twenty-four hours since then, Zach had done more than his share of fantasizing about exactly what he wanted to do with her next time they were alone. Not that there would be a next time.

Tell that to his body. A fresh wave of desire hit him; it was so strong that he got hard just sitting there. Lucky for him, the booth hid his lap.

Curly shot a puzzled look at both of them. "Uh, you want to join us?"

Just what Zach needed—the company of the woman he was better off avoiding.

"Actually, I'm here to pick up an order," she said. "If it's not ready, I'll sit down for a minute—if it's okay with you, Zach."

It was so not okay, but he shrugged. "Sure."

While she was gone to check on the order, Curly raised his eyebrows. Ignoring him, Zach helped himself to another wedge of pizza.

Moments later, Gina returned to the table. "My pizzas are still in the oven. The guy at the counter will call my name when they're ready."

"You ordered more than one, eh?" Curly said. "Is your family coming over tonight?"

Gina shook her head. "They're for a party at Autumn Naylor's house."

"Hope Ranch." Curly nodded. "I've been in that house. It's nice and big, perfect for a party."

Zach pictured people milling around, some of them no doubt trolling for available women. The thought of a bunch of single men scoping out Gina bothered him. "Who else will be there?" he asked, narrowing his eyes.

She looked surprised by the question. "Friends from high school who are home for Thanksgiving break and a few other people."

Curly laughed. "Cody's cool. I'll bet he wouldn't mind if Zach and I crashed his party."

Gina smiled. "But Autumn would. This is a girls-only party. Cody isn't even invited."

Zach relaxed. "Did you get a lot done at the house today?"

"I did." She wouldn't meet his eyes, whether because of those kisses last night or something else, he wasn't sure. "But there's still much more to do."

"Naylor," a teenage boy called out.

"That's my order." Gina jumped out. "I'll see you later."

Zach followed her with his eyes. He couldn't help it. Her camel hair coat bustled around her legs as she hurried to the pickup counter, all corporate and businesslike. He imagined she moved that quickly all the time at work.

Carrying four large boxes, she moved more slowly toward the door. Several men checked her out. Two started to rise to hold the door for her.

Zach slid out of the booth and beat them to it. The scent of fresh-baked pizza all but drowned out her scent, but he swore he caught a whiff of her perfume.

"Thanks," she said with a quick smile.

"No problem. You and your girlfriends have a good time tonight."

"We will. You, too."

Curly didn't say a word until the door closed behind her and Zach returned to the booth. With a wink, he leaned toward Zach. "She's interested in you."

Zach shook his head. "She goes for the corporate-executive type."

"A woman's eyes don't lie, man. Every time she glanced your way, they lit up."

So that he wouldn't have to reply, Zach bit off a huge chunk of pizza.

"I saw how you watched her when she wasn't looking," Curly went on. "Why are you even talking about going to Sparky's tonight when what you want just walked out the door?"

Zach glanced out the large front window. He could see Gina piling the pizza boxes in the passenger seat of Lucky's truck, her thick coat hiding her hips. All the same, he was aroused. He tore his gaze away and cleared his throat. "Maybe I don't want to be interested in her."

"Doesn't mean you aren't."

"She's not my type."

"Come on, man. She's beautiful and a lot hotter than the brunette at the other table. By the way, as soon as she saw the way you looked at Gina, she left."

Curly's plate was empty. "You finished?" Zach asked. When his friend nodded, he said, "Me, too. I changed my mind about that beer. I'm ready to call it a night."

"It's only seven-thirty, man. Let's grab a pitcher at Sparky's like we talked about."

Zach didn't feel like it anymore. "When we get back, you go on without me."

"Suit yourself. But it's gonna be one lame Saturday night for you."

## Chapter Eight

Feeling like a giant bundle of exposed nerves, Gina set the pizzas on the passenger seat of the truck. She could feel Zach looking at her—or was she imagining things? On the way to the driver's side of the car, she glanced furtively through the front window of the Pizza Palace. He was frowning at Curly, almost as deeply as he'd frowned at her when she'd walked through the door.

He'd been less than pleased to see her tonight, and apparently he was still unhappy. Gina hadn't exactly been thrilled to see him, either. She pulled out of the parking lot and turned onto the highway. She hadn't expected to see him for several days and hadn't been prepared for the powerful effect his mere presence had on her.

The heat and naked need on his face had stirred her own desire. It was a good thing he hadn't unleashed his smile. Because if he had, she'd probably still be sitting in that booth, wanting him.

Which was startling in itself. No man had ever made her feel like that, turning her on with just a look.

Out of all the available men in the world, why did she have to want Zach Horton?

Refusing to think about him anymore tonight, Gina turned on the radio. The toe-tapping music from the blue-grass country station reminded her of Uncle Lucky, and she suffered a wistful pang. He'd loved bluegrass. At the same time, the delicious smells of freshly baked pizza filled the truck, making her mouth water. Better to salivate over food than Zach.

In what seemed like no time, she was rolling up the long gravel driveway of Hope Ranch. Although she'd never been there before, even when it had been known as Covey Ranch, she was aware that Hope Ranch was far more successful than the Lucky A.

That was obvious by the big house alone. Light blazed from every window on the main floor and across the wraparound porch, making for an impressive sight.

A good half dozen cars were parked in a large turn-around near the house. Gina parked the truck there. Cradling the pizza boxes, she climbed the steps and crossed the porch. She rang the doorbell with her elbow.

Autumn opened the door with a smile. "I'm so glad you're here," she said, relieving Gina of the pizzas. "Thanks for picking these up."

Gina stepped into a wide entry. She shrugged out of her coat and hung it in the coat closet. In the adjoining great room seven women sat before a roaring fire. Three were friends she'd lost touch with after high school and the other three had been at the funeral. She didn't know the slightly older woman.

She needed this night, catching up with old friends and getting better acquainted with new ones. She needed to relax and push Zach, Uncle Lucky's death and her work worries from her mind.

The women smiled and called out greetings, and immediately Gina felt at home.

"Cocktails and appetizers are on the side table," Autumn said. "Help yourself. I'll stick these pizzas in the oven to stay warm. I'll be right back."

By the time Gina poured herself a glass of wine and found a seat on the massive sectional sofa that faced the fireplace, Autumn had returned.

She reintroduced everyone. "You remember Sarah Hollyer, Meg Dawson, her sister-in-law, Jenny, and Stacy Engle. They were all at your house the other night and at the funeral. Next to Stacy is Joan Tyee, who you haven't met. She's a close friend of mine." Autumn grinned. "When I took the housekeeping job here, I was an awful cook. Joan saved me by teaching me how to make a few things. If she hadn't, I probably wouldn't have been here long enough for Cody to fall in love with me."

"Not true." Joan's eyes sparkled. "He was in love with you the second you walked into the house."

"Joan's husband, Doug, is foreman here at Hope Ranch," Autumn said. "He's really great with our foster sons."

Gina wondered what it was like, being a foreman's wife. "Do you also work at the ranch?" she asked Joan.

The woman shook her head. "I'm an office manager for an insurance company in town. I also have two little ones at home—and as you can see, baby number three will arrive in a few months."

Joan bracketed one side of her mouth with her hand, as if about to reveal a secret she didn't want others to hear. "I'm almost forty-two," she said with a wry expression. "And this pregnancy came as a complete surprise. Doug and I are thrilled, of course."

A special glow lit Joan from the inside. Gina almost envied her, which was odd. She was so not ready for motherhood. Maybe after she was promoted to vice president—provided she met her Mr. Right.

Joan went on. "Dr. Mark assures us that everything is

normal, for which we're grateful. But after this one, I'm getting my tubes tied."

Everyone laughed.

When Meg, who was sitting next to Gina, got up to chat with someone across the room, Sarah Hollyer took her place. "I've been wanting to ask you something."

Assuming she had some marketing questions, Gina smiled. "Fire away."

"What do you think of Zach?"

Taken off-guard, Gina struggled for an answer besides, *He's a great kisser.* For the life of her, she couldn't come up with anything else. "What do you mean?" she finally said.

"I met him a couple years ago, when I interviewed him and Lucky for an article I was writing about ranching in eastern Montana. Your uncle made me laugh, but Zach really impressed me with his smarts. I think he's a great guy and really good-looking. Not as handsome as Clay, but a close second."

"Uncle Lucky had quite a sense of humor," Gina said. "And you're right about Zach. He's a good man." Maybe Sarah could tell her something about him. "What do you know about his background?"

"Only that he's from Texas and has been here about three years."

"I remember when he stopped at the clinic for a tetanus shot a few months ago," Stacy said. "Every woman in the room was fanning herself. A gorgeous guy like that... It's a wonder some lucky woman hasn't snapped him up."

Gina didn't like that idea at all. Frowning, she stood. "I need more wine."

When she returned to her seat, a woman named Dani, who'd been in several of Gina's high school classes, angled her head toward her. "I hear you live in Chicago and that you're the assistant vice president at a big marketing company. What's that like?"

Finally, a subject Gina could sink her teeth into. "The job or Chicago?" she asked.

"Both."

"My job is pretty demanding, but I love the challenge. Chicago's great—it's big and vibrant, and there's always something to do."

"Wow," Dani said. "I'll bet they have great stores there."

"Every chain you can think of, plus a lot of great boutiques. It's a shopper's paradise. And the restaurants are amazing."

A lively discussion followed. Gina was enjoying herself. She loved the hustle and bustle of Chicago, but these women made Saddlers Prairie seem pretty darn great. Already she felt closer to them than she ever had to Lise or any of her other colleagues at Andersen, Coats and Mueller.

As for friends outside of work, she didn't really have any. And whose fault was that? She'd been so busy working that she hadn't taken the time to cultivate real friendships.

"I'm ready to eat," Autumn said. "Help me with the pizzas, Gina?"

Gina followed her into a spacious, state-of-the-art kitchen. "Wow," she said. "This is a far cry from the places we lived when we were kids."

"I know." Autumn grinned and pulled on oven mitts. "Sometimes I have to pinch myself to make sure my life isn't a dream. And I'm not talking our bank account or this house. I found the love of my life. With Cody, I'd be happy living in a shack."

Gina wasn't sure she believed that. "You've been poor.

You know you'd be worrying about how to pay the bills and feed yourselves."

"What I mean is, the house and money are just icing on the cake. Let's put these in the dining room."

As Gina helped arrange the pizzas on the dining room table, she mulled over Autumn's words. She'd never considered that love could matter so much more than money, and she certainly hadn't seen that with her parents. She wondered if they'd enjoyed each other's company before the bankruptcy.

"Dinner is served in the dining room," Autumn announced in a fake British accent that had everyone chuckling.

"Yay!" Stacy pushed herself up and rubbed her rounded belly. "You'd think that with this baby squishing my stomach, I'd never feel like eating. But, no, I want to feed my face all the time."

Fresh laughter broke out.

The lighthearted conversation was exactly what Gina needed. She relaxed as she hadn't in forever, and for a while she forgot all about Zach and the sad event that had brought her back to Saddlers Prairie.

The pizza was gone and everyone was sipping tea and enjoying brownies still warm from the oven when Autumn sat back and glanced at Gina.

"So are you dating anyone in Chicago?"

The conversation around the table stopped as everyone waited for Gina's reply. Now, that was being put on the spot, Gina thought.

"Not since my boyfriend and I broke up over the summer," she said. "The truth is, I've been too busy to even think about meeting guys. Once things slow down at work, I'm sure I'll start dating again." She crossed her fingers and, without intending to, held them up for all to see.

Autumn looked sympathetic—the last thing Gina wanted. "Don't worry about me," she said. "I'm happy."

But was she really?

"I used to think I'd never get married," Sarah said. "I certainly didn't see myself in Saddlers Prairie. Yet here I am, living on a ranch with the best husband in the world and the mother of year-old twins. I've never been happier."

She sounded a lot like Autumn.

Except for Gina, all the women were married with children, and they nodded and smiled. She felt like the odd girl out. Yet she also felt accepted and liked by everyone. Not for her work accomplishments but for who she was right now. She wasn't used to that. It felt…different, in a good way.

Not long after dinner, the party wound down. At the door, Autumn hugged her. "It's been great seeing you. I wish you'd think about coming home again for Christmas."

Gina had thought she didn't want to, but now she actually considered the suggestion—for all of five seconds. No, she decided. She needed to stay in Chicago and work.

Next year, for sure.

GINA SPENT SUNDAY cleaning out the basement. She stopped in time to shower and change before heading to dinner at Sophie and Gloria's. By the time she parked in front of their little house, she was hungry and grouchy. Scooping up a cake—the last of the desserts brought to the house by people paying their respects—and her parents' bankruptcy folder, she made her way to the front door. Tonight, she wanted answers.

She knocked before opening the door and stepping into the modest living room. Wonderful smells greeted her, and she sniffed appreciatively.

"There's my favorite niece." Seated in the recliner, Uncle Redd waved. "Is that a cake?"

"Your only niece," she corrected, placing her things on a chair and hanging up her coat. "And yes, it's a cake."

Her uncle frowned. "You don't look happy. Rough day?"

"Actually, I accomplished quite a bit." She had the bulging trash bags to prove it. "But no, I'm not very happy. Follow me into the kitchen and I'll explain why."

In the small kitchen, her cousins were working their magic.

"Hello," Sophie called out, tipping her cheek up for a kiss. "Dinner's almost ready."

Gloria nodded. "Grab an apron and dress the salad."

"Not until we talk."

"But dinner's almost ready," Sophie said.

"It can wait." Gina gestured at the kitchen table. "Sit." She jerked her chin at Uncle Redd. "You, too."

"Oh, dear," Gloria muttered. "What is it this time?"

"First, you neglect to warn me that instead of Uncle Redd inheriting the Lucky A, I am. I thought the secrets were behind us, but I was wrong." She slapped the thick folder on the table so that they could all see it. "I can't believe you all didn't tell me about my parents' bankruptcy."

Uncle Redd scratched the back of his neck. "It was a long time ago, honey. Before you were even born."

"According to the paperwork, I was a few months old."

"Same difference. By the time you were big enough to understand, your folks had put it behind them. What would have been the point of opening that old wound?"

"The point is, they're my parents. Bankruptcy is a huge thing, and I should've been told."

"You know now, and what good has it done?" Gloria shook her head. "You're all upset."

"I'm angry, but not because of the bankruptcy. Because of the secrecy around it."

"Your parents were ashamed—we all were," Sophie said.

Uncle Redd nodded. "We've never been rich, but we always pay our way. It's a matter of pride. That bankruptcy was the first time anyone in our family faced financial ruin. And in such a public way. Beau and Marie wanted to protect you from the shame."

In a public way? "You're saying that people in Saddlers Prairie knew?"

Her uncle nodded. "By law, *The Saddlers Prairie News* is required to print a statement as a notice to creditors. That's a requirement of anyone declaring bankruptcy. You can imagine the humiliation."

In a town the size of Saddlers Prairie, Gina definitely could. The truth was, bankruptcy was humiliating, period—even in a bustling city the size of Chicago. She was beyond thankful for her upcoming bonus.

"I never heard even a whisper about it from anyone in town," she said.

"Why would you? It was no one's business."

"But news travels around here like wildfire."

"Yes, and then it dies down."

"Tell me how it happened."

Uncle Red rested his arms on the table. "Beau wasn't frugal like Lucky and me. He had a reckless streak and liked to spend money."

"He used to say that if you spend like you're rich, then you'll be rich," Gloria said. "He claimed that was how he got your mama to look at him and her daddy to bring him into the farm-equipment business."

Gina nodded. "He was dressing for success." When her family gave her blank looks, she explained. "In the corporate world, looking and acting successful is key to real success. People treat you differently and doors open that would otherwise stay closed."

"Beau may have taken over the business, but he wasn't anything like a corporate executive," Uncle Redd said. "He spent his paycheck on trips to Vegas and things he didn't need. A big truck, a fancy car for Marie, a new color TV and whatever else caught his fancy."

Gloria made a face. "As you can imagine, on Beau's salary that didn't work out so well. He opened a few credit cards and got him and Marie into a real financial pickle. Back then, he handled the finances. Marie had no idea that they were living on credit. She thought they were doing real well, and Beau did everything he could to keep her believing it. After they declared bankruptcy, she closed all the credit-card accounts and took over the budget."

"So that's why Dad had to ask Mom for any money he wanted to spend," Gina said.

"Uh-huh." Uncle Redd shook his head. "Beau didn't like that one bit, but it was either toe Marie's line or hit the road, Jack."

"Were they ever happy together?"

"Until your mom found out about the financial mess he'd gotten them into."

No longer angry, Gina sighed. "If I'd known all that, I would've understood my parents a whole lot better." Though her life wouldn't have been any easier.

"Are we finished here?" Gloria asked. "Because I'd like to eat sometime before midnight."

"Okay, but first, are there any other secrets I should know about? If so, please tell me now. I don't want to come across papers someplace and get sucker punched again."

Her relatives looked genuinely thoughtful for a moment. Then they glanced at each other and shrugged.

"None that I can think of," Uncle Redd said.

Sophie shook her head. "If something comes to me, I promise I'll tell you."

"Girl Scouts' honor." Gloria held up her hand in a three-finger salute.

"If you don't, I'll never trust any of you again." Gina grabbed an apron from a kitchen drawer. "Now I'll dress that salad."

## Chapter Nine

At eight o'clock sharp Monday morning—nine o'clock Chicago time—Gina called the office.

"Good morning," Marsha said in her cheerful voice. "How are things in Montana?"

Gina thought of Zach and the old and new friends she'd made. "Not bad, considering."

"All ready for Thanksgiving?"

"No, but I will be." With Sophie and Gloria's help, she'd put together a grocery list for the holiday. After she cleaned out Uncle Lucky's bedroom today, she would head to Spenser's and buy the needed ingredients. "How about you?"

"Haven't started yet. I'm awfully glad we're closed on Wednesday. I need that day to buy groceries and cook. I imagine Carrie told you she's sick?"

"Sick?" Gina echoed.

"She just called in—I assumed she'd talked to you first. She has the flu and a bad case of laryngitis. I could barely hear a word she said. She won't be in today, and I doubt she'll be in tomorrow, either."

Gina had checked her email before going to Gloria and Sophie's the night before and had seen Carrie's report and an email that had been upbeat and relieved her worries.

But now… The fact that her assistant hadn't contacted her was both puzzling and worrisome.

Especially with a busy day scheduled. She rubbed the space between her eyes. "Meetings with Evelyn Grant and another client are set up for this afternoon, and I'm going to need help. Who's in the office?"

"Everyone but Carrie and Kevin. He's out for the day with potential new clients. The rest are all in back-to-back meetings, but Shirley and Jon should be finished around three. Shall I buzz one of them?"

Both colleagues worked as hard as Gina, and she doubted they had time to step in. "Never mind," she said. "I'll call the clients and set up phone meetings instead."

"All right. If I don't talk to you again before Thursday, happy Thanksgiving. We'll be awfully glad to have you back next week."

Irritated, Gina speed-dialed Carrie's cell phone. She didn't expect her assistant to pick up, and of course, the woman didn't. "I'm sorry you're sick," Gina said when voice mail kicked in. "But we still need to talk before Thanksgiving. As soon as you feel better, give me a call— even if you have laryngitis."

She spent the next hour making calls to clients and apologizing for not returning calls the day before. They all knew about Uncle Lucky and seemed surprised that she was calling instead of Carrie. Explaining that her assistant was ill, Gina set up phone meetings for the following morning.

Then, channeling her frustration with Carrie, she attacked Uncle Lucky's bedroom.

Stacks of old catalogs filled one wall. Sweating and muttering, Gina hefted trash bags of J.C. Penney and farm and agriculture catalogs downstairs.

"What were you thinking, Uncle Lucky?" she muttered as she shoved the heavy bags outside.

They joined a mound along the back of the house—a big, ugly pile of black plastic against the snow. Hating the sight, Gina decided to burn their contents in the bin near the barn. Right away.

Then she would drive to Spenser's and pick up the groceries for Thanksgiving and another box of trash bags. She would check her email, too. After that, she might even stop at Barb's Café and treat herself to dinner.

USING ONE OF Lucky's old Jeeps to trundle from pasture to pasture, Zach kept an eye out for stranded or lost cattle. He preferred riding horses, but with the temperature somewhere south of twenty degrees, it was too damn cold. He was out of the car, battling the harsh wind and tramping down a gully to reach a misguided heifer, when he smelled smoke.

He squinted at the white plume, which looked to be coming from someplace near the barn. When he'd checked in with the crew earlier, no one had mentioned burning any trash today. That left Gina.

The heifer lowed mournfully, and Zach turned his attention to her. She'd wandered onto the icy gully bed and couldn't get across it.

He slipped and slid toward her. "Easy there," he said. Hands on her rump, he grunted and shoved, forcing her forward until her hooves found purchase. She trotted up the slope of the gully. Panting and sweating, he followed her out. When they both reached flat ground, he gave her rump a thwack. She loped off toward the rest of the herd.

One down and hopefully zero to go.

Ready to resume his search for lost cattle, he climbed into the Jeep, pulled off his gloves and cranked up the heat. But instead of heading for the back pastures, he drove toward the barn. Toward Gina.

Though acres separated them, she was easy to spot. Her burgundy jacket added color to the gray afternoon. Zach steered toward her. He hadn't seen her since running into her at the Pizza Palace Saturday night. They'd both been uncomfortable, and he figured they should probably talk. This was as good a time as any.

As he neared her, he noted the jeans hugging her long legs. Legs that fueled his fantasies and kept him up at night. She was hefting a fat black bag, one of a pile nearby. Hearing the Jeep, she paused and shaded her eyes against the winter sun. She wasn't wearing a hat or a scarf. In this weather? What was she thinking?

He watched her dump the contents of the bag into the bin. The paper caught quickly, wind fanning the flames high and whipping her hair across her face.

Braking to a stop, he exited the vehicle, shoved his hands into his jacket pockets and tromped across the snow toward her. "That's a lot of trash bags."

"You have no idea."

"You're supposed to ask for help."

"I wanted to do it myself."

She couldn't seem to keep still. She walked around the fire, fiddled with her gloves and pulled up her jacket collar. Her cheeks were red with cold. Zach could think of a few great ways to warm her up, all of them involving getting her naked and under the covers. He swallowed. "Where's your hat?"

"I left it at the house. I meant to grab a scarf, but I was distracted and forgot."

"I've got an extra wool cap in the Jeep. It isn't fancy like your hat, but at least you'll be warm."

"Great—thanks."

He retrieved the navy cap and handed it to her. She pulled on the cap so that her ears were covered. She looked cute.

"That's much better. I'll give it back later." She held out her gloved hands to the fire.

"Keep it until you leave. We need to talk about the other night," he said.

"You mean at the Pizza Palace?"

"I was thinking about a different night." The night he'd kissed her until his body was on fire. "You'll be seeing a lot of me while you're here, and I want us to be comfortable around each other."

"I'm okay, Zach. I wanted what happened."

He had to ask. "Do you want it to happen again?"

"I don't know." She poked at the fire, stirring the flames higher. "Right now, I don't know much of anything."

She looked like she needed a friend. "You want to talk about it?" he asked.

"You might be sorry you asked."

She gave a wry smile, coaxing a smile from him. He scooped up a trash bag and emptied it in the bin. Fresh flames crested the metal walls. "I'll take that risk."

"Okay, but don't say I didn't warn you," she began. "I set up a phone call with my assistant for this morning, but she's sick with the flu. She can't help that, but she didn't even bother to let me know. I found out from the office receptionist. I think she's avoiding me, and I wish I knew why."

Zach should've guessed that this was about work. "Maybe she's afraid of you."

"The way she's been acting since I left, she should be. I can't get a hold of her, and we've been communicating mostly through texts. It's almost as if she's ducking me."

Gina looked indignant. "In the six months since I hired her, she's always worked as hard as I do. She's ambitious, too, and seemed more than eager to take over for me for a few days. I wish I knew what she's up to."

"Maybe she thought she was ready for the responsibility, but she isn't. Or she's having boyfriend or husband problems and it's interfering with the job."

"She's single, and she's always been focused, no matter what. She wants to get promoted. We're a lot alike that way. Right now, she doesn't even have a boyfriend. But come to think of it, Friday night she did have a date with someone new." Gina rubbed her chin, leaving behind a smudge. "I wonder if she caught the flu from him."

"You'll find out when you get back next week. You'll straighten things out then."

"Let's hope. I can't afford to have anything else fall through the cracks." Her eyes were round and shadowed. "I really need her to pull her weight."

"What fell through the cracks?"

"Appointments with two clients—one of them a huge account. I set up phone meetings with them for tomorrow, which isn't ideal, but it's better than nothing. The problem is I don't have time for that right now. There's still so much to do with the house. I haven't emptied Uncle Lucky's closet and dresser or sorted through either of the guest bedrooms, and I have less than a week to get it done." She emptied a bag into the fire.

"Sure you don't want help?"

"You still have plenty to do. Anyway, this is something I should do on my own. Thanks for listening. There really isn't anyone else I can talk to."

"No problem." To keep the fire going, he dumped another bag onto the fire. "Lots of newspapers and magazines here."

"And old bills that go back decades. I found this stuff everywhere—stacked on shelves in the basement, in Uncle Lucky's office and in his bedroom…" Gina shook her head. "I knew he was a pack rat, but I never guessed he was this bad."

With a frown bracketing her mouth, she looked worn down, even more exhausted than when she'd stepped off the plane.

"Did you find anything worth saving?" he asked. "Something that might change your mind about holding on to this ranch?"

"You don't give up, do you?"

He made a face and she laughed, which was what he'd wanted.

Zach grinned. "Seeing you crack a smile eases the pain of your decision."

A moment later she sobered. "I wish… It's too bad you don't have the money to buy the Lucky A."

Her words just about knocked him to his knees. Not even Lucky knew that he had money—a great deal of it. It sat untouched in an investment account and had since Zach had sold his company for a hefty sum. He'd given away half of the profits but wasn't sure what to do with the rest. He didn't intend to use the money for himself.

"Even if I did, I'd never buy this place," he said. "Lucky willed it to you, and he meant for you to keep it."

"Yes, I know." Her eyes took on a stubborn glint and she set her jaw. "I'm not going to change my mind, Zach."

As determined as she seemed, he wasn't about to give up. "You never did say if you found anything in those papers."

"As a matter of fact, I did." She kicked at the snow. "Lucky kept a folder that belonged to my parents. I discovered that around the time I was born, they had de-

clared bankruptcy. I had no idea—no one ever told me."
She frowned. "I don't understand secrets like that."

Zach did. Some things were best kept from others.
"Every family has skeletons in their closet," he said.

"Yes, but do they keep those secrets from their own
flesh and blood?"

Thanks to the internet and the local paper, Zach's family and anyone who read the business pages knew about
his mistakes. He shrugged. "I guess that depends."

"Maybe. At least now I know why my mother was so
tightfisted."

She angled her head a fraction, and he knew she was
going to ask him something.

"Did your parents fight over money?"

As an insurance executive, Zach's father earned more
than he could ever spend, and his mother's trust fund
made her independently wealthy. "No, but they fought
about everything else." Remembering the constant volley
of criticism and accusations, he winced. "They divorced
and remarried each other twice before they both moved
on to other partners. My father is still with his third wife,
and my mother just married husband number four."

"And I thought my childhood was rough."

"I got used to it."

"I always wished I had a brother or sister, especially
when my parents fought. Do you have any siblings?"

"A brother, and yeah, as kids, we leaned on each other
quite a bit."

"Is he still in Texas?"

Zach nodded. "He and his wife live in Houston."

"I'll bet you miss him."

"We're not close anymore." Not since Zach had sold
his business and walked away from his life of luxury.
Jim thought he was crazy. The entire family did, and ex-

cept for obligatory phone calls on holidays, they rarely touched base.

Gina opened her mouth, no doubt to ask him something else.

Wary, he eyed her. "What's with the questions?"

"I just think we should get to know each other better."

She already knew more about him than most people in town. Zach let his eyes travel lazily over her. "After the other night, I'd say we're starting to get to know each other pretty well."

Her red cheeks flushed redder still. "You know what I mean." She didn't ask him anything else, which was what he'd intended. "I need to finish this and get to Spenser's." She emptied two trash bags into the bin, one on top of the other, jumping back when the flames flared up. She almost bumped into Zach.

"Careful." He caught her in his arms.

She'd knocked the hat cockeyed. With cold fingers, he tucked her hair back and straightened the cap, tugging it gently over her ears. "There."

His fingers lingered on her soft skin.

"Your hands are cold," she said.

"I took off my gloves when I got you the hat." Zach dropped his arms to his sides. He longed to kiss her—and more. But any of the ranch hands could be nearby. Already Curly suspected that something was going on between Zach and Gina, and Zach didn't want him or the other men catching sight of anything that would cause them to talk.

The shed where Lucky stored tractors and other heavy equipment was only a few yards away. "I want to show you something." Zach caught hold of Gina's hand and tugged her forward. "It's important."

"What is it?"

"It's important," he repeated.

## OFFICIAL OPINION POLL

Dear Reader,

Since you are a book enthusiast, we would like to know what you think.

Inside you will find a short Opinion Poll. Please participate in our Poll by sharing your opinion on 3 subjects that are very important to all of us.

To thank you for your participation, we would like to send you **2 FREE BOOKS** and **2 FREE GIFTS!**

Please enjoy them with our compliments.

Sincerely,

*Pam Powers*

# YOUR OPINION POLL
# THANK-YOU FREE GIFTS INCLUDE:

▶ **2 HARLEQUIN® AMERICAN ROMANCE® BOOKS**

▶ **2 LOVELY SURPRISE GIFTS**

## OFFICIAL OPINION POLL

**YOUR OPINION COUNTS!**
Please check TRUE or FALSE below to express your opinion about the following statements:

**Q1** Do you believe in "true love"?

*"TRUE LOVE HAPPENS ONLY ONCE IN A LIFETIME."*
○ TRUE
○ FALSE

**Q2** Do you think marriage has any value in today's world?

*"YOU CAN BE TOTALLY COMMITTED TO SOMEONE WITHOUT BEING MARRIED."*
○ TRUE
○ FALSE

**Q3** What kind of books do you enjoy?

*"A GREAT NOVEL MUST HAVE A HAPPY ENDING."*
○ TRUE
○ FALSE

**YES!** I have placed my sticker in the space provided below. Please send me the **2 FREE books** and **2 FREE gifts** for which I qualify. I understand that I am under no obligation to purchase anything further, as explained on the back of this card.

### 154/354 HDL F4XP

FIRST NAME

LAST NAME

ADDRESS

APT.#

CITY

STATE/PROV.

ZIP/POSTAL CODE

HAR-1F-IU/13
Printed in the U.S.A. © 2013 HARLEQUIN ENTERPRISES LIMITED.
® and ™ are trademarks owned and used by the trademark owner and/or its licensee.

# ⬡ HARLEQUIN® READER SERVICE—Here's How It Works:

BUSINESS REPLY MAIL
FIRST-CLASS MAIL    PERMIT NO. 717    BUFFALO, NY

POSTAGE WILL BE PAID BY ADDRESSEE

HARLEQUIN READER SERVICE
PO BOX 1341
BUFFALO NY 14240-8571

NO POSTAGE
NECESSARY
IF MAILED
IN THE
UNITED STATES

If offer card is missing write to: Harlequin Reader Service, P.O. Box 1867, Buffalo NY 14240-1867 or visit www.ReaderService.com

"Is it okay to leave the fire?"

With the ground covered in snow and no trees within fifty feet, there was no danger of a spread. He nodded and tugged her toward the shed.

Moments later, they stood on the far side of the building, out of view of prying eyes.

Gina looked around and frowned. "I don't see anything here except snow. What did you want to show me?"

"It's this way."

Never taking his eyes from her, he backed her toward the siding. The curious look on her face quickly changed to something altogether different. Pure yearning.

When she was trapped between the shed and him, he placed his hands on either side of her head and kissed her.

She hesitated briefly, and then let out the soft little moan that drove him wild, placed her gloved hands around his neck and pulled him closer. Or tried. Thanks to their bulky coats, they barely touched.

That didn't stop Zach from catching fire. He wanted to drag her to the nearest bed, get naked and bury himself in her warmth. But that wasn't a good idea. Reluctantly, he broke the kiss.

"Let me know if you want help with the house," he said.

Nodding, she stood where she was, against the wall, flushed and dreamy eyed, and watched him walk away.

## Chapter Ten

One down, one to go, Gina thought as she hung up from a phone meeting Tuesday morning. The next call, to Evelyn Grant, was scheduled for an hour from now. With so much to do before leaving town, she wasn't about to waste a minute. She decided to empty Uncle Lucky's bedroom dresser and closet, which shouldn't take long.

Aside from well-worn jeans and flannel shirts, he didn't have a lot. Most of the clothing was ready for the rag bin, but a few items were in good enough condition for charity. She set those aside, along with his boots, which were in decent shape. His old Stetson sat on the shelf above the clothing rod.

At the sight of the battered hat, Gina's eyes filled. She couldn't part with that, so she set it aside, along with two photos. In one, she was about eight and seated on Belle, a gentle old workhorse, while a young-looking Uncle Lucky grinned by her side. The other was of her uncle and Zach on the roof of the barn, replacing the roof. Obviously mugging for the photographer, they held up tools and grinned against a cloudless blue sky.

In a white T-shirt and faded jeans, Zach looked gorgeous. A man didn't come by those biceps and flat belly without engaging in serious physical labor.

He was pretty serious about kissing, too....

Gina went all soft inside, caught herself and raised her chin. Zach wasn't what she wanted, and she was not going to kiss him again.

Setting the hat and photos aside, she reached for an ancient shoe box on the shelf. Men's dress shoes—she didn't remember her uncle ever wearing those. But the box weighed too little to contain shoes, and she heard the familiar rustle of papers inside.

"Oh, dear God, not more to sort through," she muttered.

Dreading what she'd find, she pulled the lid off. The box was filled with letters. A whole stack of them, addressed to her uncle in neat, feminine script Gina didn't recognize.

The top envelope showed a faded postage stamp marked Red Deer, a town about forty miles away. The date was some thirty years ago, when she'd been a newborn and Uncle Lucky was in his mid-forties.

Curious, she sat down on the floor with the box, opened the envelope and slid out a folded, multiple-page letter.

The faint scent of rose perfume filled her nostrils. That and the *My Dearest Lucky* greeting had her eyes opening wide.

Apparently her seemingly celibate uncle had once had a girlfriend.

"Well, well, Uncle Lucky." Wanting to know more, she went straight to page three, where the letter ended with, *I can't wait until next Saturday night. Love, Corinne.* Beside the signature was a hot-pink lipstick imprint. "Corinne with the sexy lips," Gina murmured, smiling.

She'd never heard her uncle mention anyone by that name, but then he'd never mentioned a girlfriend, period.

According to the postage-stamp dates, her uncle had received weekly letters from Corinne for three years. Wanting to know why the letters had stopped and everything in between, Gina found the first letter and started reading.

Corinne had sent a thank-you for the birthday flowers Uncle Lucky had brought her on her twenty-seventh birthday. She'd been quite a bit younger than he.

She wasn't a great writer, but her stories about the animals treated at the large veterinary clinic where she worked made for entertaining reading. Corinne's insights and feelings about Uncle Lucky made the letters even more interesting, and Gina read them all. The last one, written shortly before Corinne's thirtieth birthday, broke Gina's heart. Corinne wrote that she was tired of waiting for Uncle Lucky to propose and ended the relationship.

He could've married and had kids. Kids that would be Gina's age and would probably have wanted to keep the Lucky A. Instead, he'd died childless and alone.

With a heartfelt sigh, Gina set the box aside. Suddenly she remembered. The phone meeting with Evelyn Grant! She'd completely forgotten.

She grabbed her phone and called Ms. Grant's private line. "Evelyn Grant," said the crisp voice.

Gina swallowed. "Good morning, Ms. Grant, it's Gina Arnett. I, uh, I'm running a little late today, and I apologize. But I'm ready now and—"

"A *little* late? We scheduled our meeting for nearly an hour ago."

Having never forgotten something so important in her life and never let anything come between her and her clients—especially this one—Gina felt both terrible and embarrassed. Her face burned with humiliation. "I'm so sorry. Do you have time now?"

"Kevin and I have already spoken."

That was not good. As if on cue, Gina's other line

buzzed impatiently. Kevin, the screen read. He would have to wait.

"Again, I am so sorry," she said. "What can I do to make this up to you?"

"Don't blow me off ever again."

The phone clicked harshly in Gina's ear.

Groaning, she buried her face in her hands. Not ready to face Kevin, she phoned her favorite Chicago florist and ordered the most expensive Thanksgiving flower bouquet available to be sent to Evelyn Grant immediately.

Then, biting the bullet, she called her boss and apologized.

Kevin's disapproving silence screamed in her ear.

"I sent flowers," she added lamely.

"That doesn't make up for what you did. Grant Industries is one of our biggest clients, Gina. They represent substantial fees for us. Someone else could've taken over the account while you're out, but you insisted that you and Carrie could handle it. What's going on with her? Since you left she's hardly been at the office. You should've let me know she was falling short."

He'd trusted Gina to do her job and she'd let him down.

"If we lose the account because of your mistakes…" Kevin let the incomplete threat hang in the air.

Knowing she was in trouble, Gina winced. "You have my word that I'll make this up to you and Evelyn Grant."

"You'd damn well better."

"I'll be in the office bright and early Monday morning, and everything will be fine," she assured him.

"It had better be."

In other words, her job was on the line. Kevin wasn't the most understanding boss. She'd seen people fired for less.

He hung up, the click of his phone sounding ominous—exactly like Evelyn Grant's.

EARLY ON THANKSGIVING DAY Zach turned up the Lucky A driveway, the twenty-pound tom turkey he'd picked up from a rancher in another town tucked safely on the passenger seat of the truck. He looked forward to the great meal and the relaxing day ahead, but first there were chores that needed doing. He also needed to change clothes. Which was why he planned to drop off the bird at the house and come back later.

He was near the parking area by the back door when his cell phone rang. He glanced at the screen. It was his brother, Jim. Zach hadn't spoken to him since May, when he'd called to wish Zach a happy birthday.

He braked to a stop. "Hey, Jim."

"Hey," his brother said. "Happy Thanksgiving."

"Back at ya. When are you and Susan taking the kids to Dad and Ava's for Thanksgiving dinner?"

"Four. I'll bet you're eating with the Arnetts again, watching a bowl game and enjoying the good company."

Jim sounded envious. "That's right." Zach wasn't going to say anything, but the words slipped out. "It won't be like last year, though. Lucky had a heart attack last week. He didn't make it."

"That was unexpected."

Zach cleared his throat. "Yeah."

"I'm sorry. So your Thanksgiving will be as dismal as mine."

Zach snorted. "I seriously doubt that."

"You're probably right. What are you going to do now that Lucky is gone?"

He wasn't about to explain about his promise to Lucky or about Gina. "I'll be here at the ranch for a while, tying up loose ends."

"Are you coming home, then?"

"I'm already here. Saddlers Prairie is my home now."

"Compared to Houston, that little burg has nothing to offer. Come back, Zach. It's time to stop punishing yourself for something that wasn't your fault."

"I'm not punishing myself." Anymore. "A man can change, and I did. I'm a rancher now. Why can't you and the rest of the family accept that?"

"Because you have an MBA from Harvard, and you built and ran a successful commercial real-estate business. That's why."

"A business I sold."

"For a hefty profit, and I respect that. People buy and sell businesses all the time. Start a new enterprise. Hell, ranches are businesses, too. If you bought one and ran it, I might understand. But you're working for someone else, and all your smarts and know-how are going to waste."

They'd hashed through this umpteen times. Zach was in no mood to do it again. He snorted. "You sound more like Dad every day."

"Don't play the Dad card on me. You know I want you to be happy."

Zach thought about his life on the ranch, the hard physical labor and the feeling of accomplishment at the end of the day. "I am," he said. "Send my love to Susan and the kids."

"Conversation over—I get the message. Susan and the kids send their love back. You going to call Dad and Ava and wish them a happy Thanksgiving?"

Zach glanced at the lit kitchen window, which was all steamed up from whatever the family was cooking. He wanted to get in there, drop off the turkey, do his chores and hurry back. "Maybe later."

In a far darker mood now, he pocketed the phone, plucked the turkey off the seat and stepped onto the back stoop. He wiped his feet and knocked before opening the door and stepping into the kitchen. "I'm here to drop off the turkey. Where do you want it?"

"You're just in time," Gina said. She was standing at the stove, stirring something. "My cousins are making the stuffing now."

In a plaid bib apron, she looked like a glamorous cooking show host—if you didn't count the forced smile and circles under her eyes. Looked as if she still wasn't sleeping well. Probably worried about something job related.

She wasn't the only one. Sunday morning she was leaving, and Zach still hadn't managed to change her mind about the ranch. He needed a plan, but hadn't come up with one.

"Ladies." He nodded at Sophie and Gloria, who sat at the table, each chopping vegetables on portable cutting boards.

Sophie patted her hair and smoothed the bib of her own apron, as if wanting to look her best for him, and Gloria offered a flirtatious smile that would probably knock a seventy-something guy off his feet. Behind them, Gina shook her head, as in, what can you do with these two?

Zach couldn't stop a grin.

"Before you give that bird to Gina, show him to us," Gloria said.

Zach held the turkey up for her inspection.

Sophie nodded approvingly. "You picked out a nice fat one. What does he weigh, twenty pounds?"

"A little over."

"You did good, honey." Gloria smacked her lips. "We'll be eating leftovers for days."

"If that's a problem for you, I'm happy to help out," Zach teased, feeling better by the moment.

"You know you're invited back for leftovers, just like always," Sophie said.

The Arnetts were so different from his own family, who left their chef to cook and never shared the leftovers. "I'm counting on it. It already smells good in here."

"It should—Gina's been working for hours, making pies, sweet potato casserole and cranberry sauce," Sophie said. "We already told her that you're the official mashed potatoes and gravy expert."

Zach nodded. "That's why they invite me back every year."

Gina laughed, and a genuine smile lingered on her lips. Zach exhaled in relief and realized he'd been waiting for that.

"After Redd dropped us off here, he went to get the chestnuts," Gloria said. "But he'll be back soon. He'll want to roast them over the fire and watch the game with you."

"Then I better finish my chores, go home and clean up and come right back."

"As THANKSGIVINGS GO, this one ranks right up there with the best of them." Uncle Redd gave Gina a fond look. "It's great to have you here in the bosom of our family, honey."

"It's good to be here." Gina meant that. Surrounded by family and Zach made it easier to set aside her worries about work. "I just wish Uncle Lucky were with us."

"Oh, he's here." Gloria glanced around and smiled. "I can feel him."

Her sister sniffed. "Don't be ridiculous."

"I *do* feel him. If you don't, then I feel sorry for you."

"Well, stop."

"Girls, girls," Uncle Redd said. "We're celebrating Thanksgiving, remember?"

Gina glanced at Zach. Eyes twinkling, he shrugged.

She couldn't help laughing. "Now it sounds like the Thanksgivings I remember so fondly."

"Sure was a good meal." With cheeks that matched his name, Uncle Redd patted his round middle. "You girls outdid yourselves today, and Zach, those mashed potatoes and gravy were your best yet. Only trouble is, there's no room left in this belly for pie."

Gina chuckled along with everyone else. She'd laughed a lot today, and she felt good.

Sophie pushed her chair back. "I'd suggest a walk, but it's too cold and slippery out there. Let's digest awhile before we think about dessert."

"You all relax and I'll clean up," Zach offered. In a sports jacket and khakis, he looked handsome. He slipped out of the jacket and rolled up the cuffs of his oxford shirt. He'd eaten as much as Uncle Redd, but unlike her uncle, his cheeks weren't flushed and his belly was still flat.

"I'll help," Gina said, rising.

Gloria frowned. "You've been working all day, honey. Redd, give Zach a hand. Moving around will help your stomach settle. When you two finish, Sophie and I will make the coffee and cut the pie. For now, we girls are going to enjoy the fire in the living room." She stood and beckoned Gina and Sophie to follow her.

"That Zach is a keeper," Gloria said when the three of them were seated around the fireplace. "If only there'd been a man like him when I was your age…."

"Harvey was a fine man, Gloria. So was my Tony."

"I know that, Sophie—I'm just trying to make a point." With a devilish look on her face, she gave an exaggerated nod toward Gina.

They expected a rise out of her, but the best she could manage was a shrug.

"You don't seem your regular self, cookie," Sophie said. "All this sorting through Lucky's things has worn you out."

That was partly true, but Gina was also worried sick about her job. If Evelyn Grant asked to work with someone else in the firm, or worse, decided to leave Andersen, Coats and Mueller...

But no, Gina wasn't going to think about that now or share her uneasiness. Zach, her family and her friends in Saddlers Prairie all thought she was riding high, and she wasn't about to tell them otherwise.

"Or maybe you're not ready to go back to Chicago just yet?" Sophie went on. "Your visit certainly has flown by."

"Land sakes, Sophie, don't go sending her off early. It's only Thursday, and she's here until Sunday morning."

"I know that, Gloria! All I'm saying is that I'll hate to see her go."

"Excuse me, but I'm right here," Gina said. Tired of their bickering, she hastily changed the subject. "I found something interesting the other day that I want to show you—after we've all had our dessert and coffee."

"I hope it isn't another secret we supposedly kept from you," Gloria said. "But then, I don't think there are any more of those."

Sophie smiled. "On that, dear sister, we agree."

## Chapter Eleven

Redd set down his pie fork and blew out a breath. "My mouth wants more, but I can't eat another bite. What'd I tell you about Gina's cooking, Zach?"

"She's great." Zach sat back, rubbed his belly and grinned. "I'm in the same boat."

After finishing his chores this morning, he'd sucked it up and called his father. The stilted conversation had been worse than the one with Jim, but then he'd expected as much. He'd come to the house in low spirits, but his mood had quickly done a one-eighty.

"I'm glad you liked the meal." Gina smiled. The shadows in her eyes had completely faded, and she looked as relaxed as Zach felt. "I like to cook but never get much of a chance at home." She glanced from Zach to her uncle. "You two say you're full, but I've seen the way you eat," she teased. "In a few hours, you'll be hungry again."

"Watching football always makes me hungry." Redd raised a hopeful eyebrow at Zach. "Ready for another game?"

"No way, Jose." Gloria shook her finger at him. "One game per holiday, remember? Besides, Gina wants to share something with us—something of Lucky's she found the other day," she added, looking pained.

"Dear Lord above." Redd put the back of his hand to his forehead. "Don't tell me she's uncovered another *secret*."

"It *is* a secret, of sorts." Gina pushed to her feet. "Wait'll you see the box I found in Uncle Lucky's closet."

"Box?" Gloria frowned. "That sounds intriguing."

Zach thought so, too, but he was more fascinated by the length of leg he glimpsed as Gina climbed the stairs. He'd never seen her in a skirt until this afternoon. Her calves were every bit as shapely as he'd imagined. She was wearing hose and he wondered if she wore a garter belt or maybe thigh highs.

He itched to run his hand up her leg and find out. His body stirred, and he nearly groaned out loud.

Redd and the cousins were shooting him curious looks, and he realized he was staring at Gina as she disappeared up the steps. He tore his gaze away and stood to clear the dessert dishes.

"Leave those," Redd said. "Let's sit by the fire and wait to see what Gina found."

When Gina returned, she set an open shoe box on the coffee table.

"Those are letters." Redd squinted at the pile. "Who are they from?"

"A woman named Corinne from Red Deer. According to the letters, she and Uncle Lucky were involved for three years."

Gloria and Sophie exchanged baffled looks, and Redd shook his head. "I never heard of any Corinne. Lucky would've said something."

"I read every letter," Gina said. "He and Corinne were definitely involved."

Not once in the three years Zach had known Lucky had the old rancher been with a woman, but he'd enjoyed looking at and talking about them. Zach was glad that at one time his friend had done more than talk.

"I certainly never guessed," Sophie said.

"Nor did I." Gloria shook her head and chuckled. "And all this time, I worried that he was a closet homosexual."

Sophie looked shocked. "Gloria!"

"Well, the man never dated or any of the other things men are prone to do. You know what I mean, Zach."

About to sip his coffee, Zach choked. He shared a look at Gina, and they both bit back laughs.

Half an hour and another piece of pie later, Redd yawned. "I'm ready to go home and sleep off this meal. Girls?"

Sophie and Gloria looked equally sleepy. They both nodded.

"We'll be back tomorrow night for leftovers," Gloria said. "Of course you'll join us again, Zach."

He glanced at Gina, waiting for her okay. She nodded. "I'll be here," he said. "The roads are pretty icy tonight. Let me drive you in my truck."

Redd frowned. "I can't leave my car here. How would I get it in the morning?"

"No problem," Gina said. "I'll drive it to your house. Zach can follow me in his truck and bring me back. If that's okay with you, Zach?"

"Sure."

She gave him a look that warmed him from the inside out and filled his head with fantasies straight out of high school—making out in the dark truck and fooling around. It wasn't gonna happen, but it sure was fun to think about.

AFTER ESCORTING SOPHIE and Gloria up a treacherous walkway and safely into the house, and then dropping off Redd and his car, Zach was alone with Gina.

"I'm glad they're all home safe," she said as he pulled away from Redd's place. "The roads really are bad to-night. And the walkway here and at my cousins' place… I worry that someone will slip and fall."

Zach shared her concern. "I'll stop at both houses in the morning and scrape and salt the walks and front steps."

"Okay, but we both know that the snow and ice will only come back again."

"True, but at least they'll be able to get to the house for leftovers."

For a few moments they rode along in silence, with only the headlights lighting the dark highway. Aware of black ice, Zach made his way cautiously toward the ranch.

"My family is something else," Gina said as they crept along.

He wasn't about to risk taking his gaze off the road, but he sensed she was smiling. He shook his head and grinned. "They're characters, all right, but good people."

"And yet so irritating. The bickering between Sophie and Gloria drives me crazy."

"I'll take them over my relatives any time. My family is too stiff and formal to bicker, but they excel at sarcasm. Every holiday meal is like a competition." Just talking about it put a bad taste in Zach's mouth. "I used to get in-digestion without taking a single bite of food."

"That doesn't sound fun."

"I'd rather have a root canal."

"But you talk to them on holidays?"

He nodded. "Some things you have to do. I don't miss being there."

"I don't miss being in Chicago, either."

She'd never said that before. Zach tore his gaze from the road to glance at her. "I thought you were anxious to get back."

"I am, but I really enjoyed celebrating Thanksgiving with my family."

Zach considered the Arnetts family. But they weren't, not really. He was on his own. Driving in the darkness, he felt truly alone—or would have without Gina beside him.

"I had a great time today, too," he said.

"I needed the break."

"You've been working hard."

"Not hard enough."

Her bitter tone surprised him. He figured she'd talk about it, but she flipped on the radio instead.

In no time, he drove under the Lucky A sign.

"Are you hungry again?" Gina asked when he pulled to a stop at the back of the house.

"I could eat. You?"

"I hate to say this, but yes."

She looked so pained about that that Zach chuckled.

"Why don't you come in and have some leftovers?" Gina said. "There'll still be plenty for tomorrow and the day after that."

Not relishing returning to his trailer just yet, Zach readily agreed.

Inside, he added another log to the fire. He helped Gina unload the dishwasher and put away the clean dishes.

"Now I'm getting really hungry," she said. "Let's make turkey and cranberry sandwiches."

"We can use the dinner rolls for bread."

"You liked those?"

He nodded and licked his lips. She laughed again, making the day that much more perfect.

Sitting side by side on the sofa, they dug in, the fire crackling merrily.

"Do you know why Corinne broke things off with my uncle?" she asked after a while. "She wanted to get married, and he wouldn't commit. I think that's so sad. He could've had a child—someone besides me to inherit the ranch."

She almost sounded regretful. Zach couldn't help but wonder if she was beginning to have second thoughts about selling the ranch. He wasn't about to push her by asking. "Some guys just aren't wired for marriage," he said.

"What about you?"

He shrugged. "I was engaged once."

"Really?" she said, clearly surprised. "What happened, if you don't mind my asking?"

The man who'd bought the Horton Company from Zach had started dating his ex-fiancée. A year later, they'd married. Gina didn't need to know about that—she'd only ask questions Zach wasn't going to answer. "She didn't like the direction my life was taking and married someone else," he summarized.

The sharp look she gave him could've cut glass.

"What?" he said.

Gina smoothed her napkin. "Was it because you were a ranch foreman?"

"There's nothing wrong with what I do, but back then, I didn't even know what a ranch foreman was."

"Where did you work?"

"It's not important. Turns out, I like being single."

Zach saw that she had more questions. Before she could voice them, he asked one of his own. "What about you, Gina? Are you a commitmentphobe?"

"Not at all, but I've been so busy working that I really haven't had time to date. I thought things might work out with my last boyfriend, but it turned out that we didn't have much in common. We didn't have great chemistry, either."

"You and I have chemistry." Zach took her plate and set it aside. "Lots of it."

When he leaned in for a kiss, she didn't stop him. One kiss wasn't enough—for either of them. He was already hard and aching, but then, just looking at her aroused him.

He cupped her soft, full breasts. He brushed his thumbs over her nipples and felt them sharpen, heard her suck in her breath and release it in a sweet, low moan.

He wanted to hear that again. Wanted her under him, begging for more. He unbuttoned her blouse. She was helping him get rid of it when he heard the landline ring.

Gina frowned. "Who'd call at ten-thirty on Thanksgiving—and on the landline? Nobody uses that except my family...." Face paling, she shrugged back into her blouse and jumped up. "Oh, God, I hope nothing's wrong."

She hurried to the kitchen, buttoning the blouse on the way. Zach was right behind her.

Reaching across the counter, she snatched up the phone. "Hello? Uncle Redd—hi. Is everything okay?" She sent Zach a worried look. "You think you're having a *heart attack?*"

Please, not Redd, too.

"Did you call Dr. Mark?" She listened. "That's good. I'm relieved that the medics are on their way. You wait for them and don't move an inch. Zach and I will be right over."

By the time she hung up, Zach had his coat on and his keys in hand.

SOME FIVE HOURS later, Gina let out an exhausted yawn and tucked Uncle Redd into his own bed. "I'm awfully glad you only had indigestion. No more overindulging, okay?"

He gave a sheepish nod. "A fifty-mile round-trip drive

to Flagg Memorial hospital in Elk Ridge is no fun, especially late at night. Sorry I bothered you and Zach."

She glanced at Zach, standing back out of the way. His eyes were hot and his expression intense, and she knew he was remembering what they'd been doing when her uncle's call had come in.

Zach's mouth on hers, his hands… If not for the interruption, she might have done something she regretted. "That's okay, Uncle Redd. You get some sleep, all right? Zach and I will be back in the morning to check on you and clean your walkway."

"Okay, honey. I still get to come to dinner tomorrow night, right?"

"Of course, but you're only allowed a small sliver of pie. Sleep tight." She kissed his whiskery cheek.

She and Zach left. "I'm sure relieved he's okay," he said as he pulled away from the curb.

So was Gina. "I'm glad I was here for him. Can you imagine going through all those tests alone? Sophie and Gloria don't drive in the dark, and I wouldn't want them to." She'd phoned her cousins several times, first to tell them what was happening and later with the results of the tests. "I don't ever want to be away again during a family emergency."

"If and when something happens, the only way you can be sure of being here is by moving back to Saddlers Prairie," Zach said.

He was right, but she was happy living in Chicago. "You don't quit, do you?"

"As the poet said, 'I have promises to keep.'"

"I'm not going to live here, but I do intend to visit more often." She would come back in the spring to check on the ranch—if it hadn't sold by then—and again next Christmas. Though the thought of celebrating a family Christmas somewhere besides the Lucky A was unbearably sad.

At almost 4:00 a.m., it was already Friday. Only two more days until she flew back to Chicago. She would miss everyone, including Zach. Especially him.

Want to or not, she liked him. A lot more than she should.

She was silently chiding herself for letting him kiss her and more when he pulled up close to the back door and set the brake. With country music softly playing on the radio, he kissed her—a long hot kiss that erased all rational thoughts and left her aching for more.

He pulled back. Reluctantly, she opened her eyes.

"Sleep tight, Gina," he said in a low, throaty voice that stroked her like a caress.

Her whole body quivered. "You, too," she managed, doubting that she'd calm down enough to sleep for a long time.

## Chapter Twelve

Zach's alarm went off Friday morning, waking him from an erotic dream involving him and Gina and a big, rumpled bed. His body was hard and pulsing, and he groaned—both from fatigue and from waking up to the reality of a double bed with only him in it.

He wanted to fall back to sleep, but Chet, Pete and Bert were gone over the holiday and this was Curly's morning to sleep in. Someone had to get up and do the chores. Grumbling, he padded into the bathroom for a shower and shave. After a quick breakfast, he headed for the barn. Snow swirled around him, stinging his face. It was still dark and he couldn't see the sky, but the air felt wet, heavy and cold. They were in for a big snow.

To his surprise, Curly was waiting for him in the barn, a steaming mug between his hands. "I didn't expect to see you up this morning," he said.

"Couldn't sleep. How was your Thanksgiving?"

Zach thought about all that had happened yesterday— the laughter and the great meal, kissing Gina and more. Redd's worried call had interrupted them before things went too far, and he was both relieved about that and frustrated. "Good and not so good," he summarized.

He explained about the trip to the hospital. "Gina and I didn't get back until almost four in the morning."

"Huh." Curly gave a knowing nod.

"Huh, what?"

"It's that look on your face. Things between you and her must be heating up."

Not about to share any details, Zach shrugged. "Like I explained before, she's looking for a different kind of guy. Anyway, she's leaving Sunday."

"I wouldn't be so sure about that. The weather people are forecasting a bitch of a storm. We're talking a mammoth blizzard."

Of all the weekends for a storm—and for Bert, Pete and Chet to be away. Zach swore. "We'd best start getting the cattle fed and into the west pasture, where the trees will give them more shelter."

Moving the stock took a while. They didn't finish until after midafternoon. Not long after they'd fed and stabled the horses, the wind picked up and the snowfall grew heavier, until Zach could barely see his own hands. With the cattle sheltered and fed for now and the horses cared for, it was time to head inside.

"Let's keep in touch," Zach said. "Have your walkie-talkie handy in case our cell phones go out. And stay warm."

Curly nodded and moved quickly toward his trailer, disappearing in the thick snow.

Zach turned toward the house. Toward Gina.

NOT LONG AFTER lunch, cupping the landline to her ear, Gina peered out the window and frowned. "Yes, Uncle Redd, it's coming down hard." So hard she couldn't see beyond the back stoop, let alone the barn. She guessed that Zach and Curly were taking care of the cattle—a huge job for only the two of them, made worse by the heavy snow.

"They're saying this will be the blizzard of the century," her uncle said.

Gina hoped they were wrong. She needed to fly home on Sunday, both to get to the office and to get away from Zach.

"It goes without saying that your cousins and I won't be over for dinner," Uncle Redd went on.

"I'll miss you, but I'm glad you're staying safe at home. Do you have enough to eat?"

"Plenty. If you need anything, don't forget that Zach is close by."

Forget? The man hadn't been out of her thoughts since she'd first opened her eyes this morning.

"Don't worry about me," she said. "I'll be fine."

"Well, I better let the dogs out to do their business while they can still get there. Call you later, honey. Or you call me."

"Will do. Love you."

With no family dinner to look forward to, the rest of Gina's day loomed heavily ahead. She hoped Zach was still planning to stop by for leftovers.

At the thought of seeing him tonight, she let out a dreamy sigh. She certainly wouldn't object to another evening of kissing and more....

"No," she firmly told herself. She couldn't.

If she were smart, she'd uninvite him to dinner, but that would be rude. She would tell him up front that there would be no kissing or anything else tonight. That made her feel safer.

If she could just stop thinking about him...

She needed to keep busy, which wasn't a problem because she still needed to clean out both of the bathrooms. She decided to start with the smaller one on the main floor.

Like all the other rooms in the house, the bathroom was cluttered with old magazines. In the linen closet she found enough towels and soap for an army. The packaging on some of the soap looked decades old, and she guessed that years ago, her thrifty Uncle Lucky had bought a case or two on sale—just as he had all those unopened office supplies. Which made her both smile and shake her head.

She decided to share the supplies with Zach and the other hands. What they didn't want, she would donate to charity. She was nearly finished, wondering whether Zach was hunkered down in his trailer or outside battling Mother Nature, when she heard a knock at the back door.

With the weather as bad as it was, it couldn't be anyone except Zach. Her heart thudding, Gina smoothed her hair, hurried to the kitchen and opened the door.

The eaves over the stoop provided some shelter, but snow coated Zach's wool face mask and coat.

"You look like a yeti," she teased, beckoning him inside.

He wiped his boots on the mat. "It's damn cold." Instead of moving into the kitchen, he stopped just inside the door. "I should tie a rope between the door and the barn so that I can find my way there later—unless you threw it away."

She shook her head. "I've been focused mostly on papers and the worthless junk Uncle Lucky saved. Whoever buys the ranch might want it and some of the tools down there. I'll get the rope."

Gina hurried down the wood steps. Moments later, rope in hand, she returned to the kitchen. "When you finish tying it, come back. I'll make a fresh pot of coffee."

He was gone awhile, so long that the coffee finished perking and started to cool. Gina was beginning to worry when he entered the house again, bringing a gust of cold air with him.

She shivered. "Perfect timing—the coffee's ready."

"Good. I need something hot."

Zach met her gaze, and her desire for him flooded back.

He pulled off his gloves, removed his boots and then shrugged out of his coat. He wore faded jeans and a thick sweater over a plaid flannel shirt.

Gina glanced out the window. "It's snowing so hard. How can you even see out there?"

"That's why I wanted the rope. I'd guess a good two feet and counting have accumulated so far. With the wind, some drifts are twice that size. And it's only been a few hours since the storm began. It's a good thing Curly and I got the cattle moved and fed."

She knew that cattle ate and drank a great deal and had to be fed and watered daily. "How will you feed them tomorrow?" she asked as she filled two mugs.

Cupping his hands around the warm ceramic, Zach carried his coffee to the table and sat down. "We'll use the plow and tractor to deliver the feed." He tasted his coffee. "While I was out there, I did some thinking. This house is much closer to the barn than my trailer. Curly's trailer is close, which is good, but he doesn't have room for me. For the sake of the cattle, I should bunk here tonight—if that's okay with you."

Zach here, all night? The very thought was unnerving, but he was right about the barn. "With two empty bedrooms upstairs and one down here, there's plenty of room, so why not?" She sat down across from him. "But no more kissing or anything else."

"I've been thinking the same thing," he said, but the heat in his gaze didn't match his words.

Her anxiety must've shown, for his mouth quirked. "Don't worry, I'll behave."

Part of her was relieved. At the same time, she also wanted him to ignore her hands-off rule. Feeling as if the devil sat on one shoulder and an angel on the other, she gave a jerky nod.

"I'll take the bedroom down here tonight."

That they would sleep on different floors felt somehow safer. Gina let out a breath. "Great."

"Great," he repeated. "Have you spoken with Redd today?"

She nodded. "A little while ago. He's fine, but with the storm, he won't be here for dinner tonight. Neither will Sophie and Gloria, and we have so many leftovers. I wish I'd given them each a plate to take home last night, but I assumed they'd be here."

"Don't worry, I'll help you get rid of the extra food." His eyes twinkling, Zach licked his lips, making her laugh.

Then she sobered. "It's a good thing the storm held off until today. Otherwise, Uncle Redd would never have gotten to the hospital and we'd all be worried sick about him." The thought made her shudder.

"He's fine," Zach said. "That's what matters."

Gina bit her lip. "I worry, though. Both my dad and Uncle Lucky had heart attacks that killed them. Uncle Redd could be next, and I'm not ready to lose him."

"Don't court trouble. If it were me, I'd schedule a physical and get him checked out."

"I'll nag Uncle Redd about that. Not that he'll listen to me."

"I'll back you up."

They lapsed into comfortable silence, like longtime friends. Or an old married couple.

Married? Gina frowned. They weren't even dating. Even if she lived here, they would never go out. They wanted different things.

She glanced out the window over the sink, where snow was rapidly accumulating on the windowsill. "How long is this storm supposed to last?"

"Days. The people on the radio are calling this the blizzard of the century."

"Well, I'm going to hope for the best," Gina said, crossing her fingers. "Big winter storms in eastern Montana aren't exactly rare, and it's a sure bet that as soon as the snow stops, the transportation people will clear the roads. By Sunday, everything should be fine."

"I wouldn't count on it."

She couldn't be stuck here! She needed to prove herself at work. "This is a really crucial time of year for my clients, Zach. I have to get home."

"Fine, but you can't control Mother Nature. Your boss knows that. He'll understand."

Under normal circumstances, maybe, but with her recent screwups and Kevin already upset, Gina had her doubts. She didn't even want to think about Evelyn Grant.

The storm had to stop, and soon. She closed her eyes and prayed for a miracle.

"Look what we did tonight," Zach said, gesturing at what was left of the turkey and trimmings. "We made a huge dent in the leftovers. Sophie, Gloria and Redd would be proud."

He waited for Gina to laugh or at least crack a smile, but the corners of her lips barely lifted. Come to think of it, she hadn't eaten all that much. She seemed nervous, really uptight.

Zach looked her straight in the eyes. "I said I wouldn't make a pass at you tonight, and I won't."

"I know." The smile she attempted fell short.

"Well, something sure has you bothered."

Resting her chin on her fist, she gave a glum sigh. "I told my boss I'd be in the office Monday morning. I want to be there, *need* to be there, but I'll probably be stuck here."

With those words, Zach knew with a sick certainty that she would never change her mind. No matter what he did or said—and because of the promise to Lucky, he wasn't about to give up—she wasn't going to hold on to the ranch.

"You really hate being here," he said.

"It's not that bad. But there's so much to do at work, and without Wi-Fi, working from here is difficult at best. I have to get to the office, where I have easy access to the internet and can run over and see my clients at any time."

Been there, done that. Only after quitting the rat race had Zach realized that most of what he'd once considered important was meaningless busywork. He doubted Gina wanted to hear that, but he could change her perspective.

"What's the worst that could happen if you stay here a few extra days?" he asked.

"Probably nothing." She toyed with her fork. "I just… There's a lot on my plate right now."

"Which your capable assistant can handle. Tell her to shape up and get it done."

Gina gave an uncertain nod. "If I can ever reach her."

"Hey." Zach tipped up her chin. "You can't do anything about it tonight, so you may as well relax."

"I'll try." She took a deep breath, exhaled and then rolled her shoulders.

"Feel better now?"

"A little. I talk to you about my worries, Zach. Why don't you talk to me?"

He frowned. "About what?"

"Anything. Your family, your past."

This was why he avoided relationships. "I told you about my family—we don't get along. As for the past, it's over and done with, so why rehash it?"

"Because it's interesting. I want to know where you used to work and what you did for a living. Why are you so closemouthed about it?"

"Because it's none of your damn business." Zach crossed his arms and set his jaw.

"All right." Gina threw up her hands. "Forget I asked."

Ready to do exactly that, he stood. "Let's get this mess cleaned up. You clear the table and I'll wash the dishes."

They worked well together and finished in no time.

Now what?

With hours left before bedtime and no fooling around on the agenda, the rest of the evening stretched out like an empty highway.

Zach thought of something to do that was both fun and safe. "Now and then, Lucky and I used to play board games," he said. "How about a game of Scrabble and a couple beers in front of the fire? We can set up the card table."

Gina perked right up. "I used to play with Uncle Lucky, too. I haven't played a board game for ages. I put those games in the giveaway pile and was going to take them to the charity box at the church. I'm glad I haven't had time."

Ten minutes later, Zach was sitting across the folding table from Gina, with two bottles of beer and the Scrabble board between them and a dictionary and score pad within easy reach.

They chose letters, and then drew to see who went

first. Gina won that. Without hesitation she spelled the word *socks*.

"That's a double score for me—twenty-two points," she said, looking pleased with herself.

Zach was impressed by her speed. As the game progressed, she grew more animated, and at last the tension that had been with her for hours faded.

Her vocabulary, competitive spirit and wit dazzled him. With the sparkle in her eyes and the flush of excitement on her cheeks, she was stunning.

Beauty, brains and a great sense of humor—talk about a lethal combination. Zach wanted her more than ever. He wanted to kiss the smug look right off her face and make her forget all about their word competition, but he'd promised not to go there.

He narrowed his eyes. "You never said you were an ace Scrabble player. You're beating the pants off me."

"That I am," she crowed. "I love to win."

"Who doesn't?" He spelled out a thirty-pointer.

"Not bad, Horton." She clamped a pen between her teeth, reminding him of a gambler with his stogie. "Would you care to bet on the winner of this game?"

Chuckling, he shrugged. "You're on. If I beat you, you have to make me breakfast when I get back from my chores in the morning. If I lose, I'll cook for you."

"Deal—and FYI, I like my eggs over easy." She reached across the table and they shook on it.

Things got serious then, both of them concentrating. By the time they were down to four tiles each, Gina was ahead by eight points.

After studying the board, she sighed. "All I can do is use my *t* and *h* to make *the*. That's four more points, giving me a twelve-point lead, minus two points for my last two tiles. Which means I win. Yes!" She pumped her fist in the air.

"Not so fast. I still have a few usable tiles left." Zach went for a triple word score. *"Kiss,"* he said with glee. "That's twenty-four points, minus two points for my last tile. I'm the winner."

"By twelve points. Darn you." Gina attempted a forbidding frown, but her laughing eyes ruined the effect.

The urge to pull her close grabbed Zach hard, and it was all he could do to stay in his seat. He scooped up the tiles and returned them to the letter bag.

Oblivious, Gina settled the lid on the box. "What time will you be back for breakfast, and what do you want to eat?"

What he wanted had nothing to do with food. "Surprise me. I don't know how long I'll be. That depends on what Curly and I find once we're out there." He stood, went to the window and looked through the drapes. "It's still coming down fast and hard."

His own words had him thinking about hard, fast sex. If he didn't get away from Gina soon, he'd break his promise for sure. He turned from the window. "I'd best get some rest."

Though as restless as he was, he'd be lucky to fall asleep anytime soon.

"I'll get you some sheets and blankets."

Gina disappeared down the hall. Zach folded up the table and chairs and pulled himself together.

When she returned, he took the bedding from her. "Tonight was fun."

"Yeah."

For a few long moments they simply stared at each other.

By the soft look in her eyes, Zach swore she wanted

him to kiss her. But she glanced away, cleared her throat and headed to her room. "Well, good night."

"Night." His unwitting gaze settled on her lush behind until she disappeared at the top of the stairs.

## Chapter Thirteen

Gina awoke to an utterly silent house, courtesy of the snow insulating the world from normal sounds. Had it finally stopped?

She hurried out of bed and peered through the blinds. The thick curtain of falling snow gave her the answer.

The storm was still raging.

Wonderful. It was after seven and Zach was probably out with the animals. Gina didn't envy him that job.

Standing under a hot shower, she thought about last night. Zach had kept her laughing. He was smart and funny and a competitive player, and she'd enjoyed spending the evening with him. A little too much.

She was starting to care about Zach a lot more than was smart.

She wanted a man with drive and ambition, she reminded herself. And though she knew a fair amount about him now, he wouldn't answer her questions about his past. What was he hiding? Whatever it was, it couldn't be good.

Her heart didn't seem to care.

Dressed in jeans and a warm pullover, she headed downstairs.

Zach had already made coffee. Grateful, she poured herself a cup and then peered out the kitchen window, hoping to catch sight of him. Gina saw only the driving snow.

Even with the rope connecting the barn and back door, navigating through the deep snow wouldn't be easy. How would Zach ever find the cattle, let alone make his way back? She began to worry.

To keep herself occupied, she wandered to the living room and flipped on the TV. Newscasters predicted record snowfall and warned people to stay inside.

In the kitchen again, she rummaged through the refrigerator and considered what to make for breakfast. Then she thumbed through the phonebook and found the number for the airport. A recording announced that it was closed and all flights were canceled until further notice. The bus station had shut down, too.

With a heavy sigh, she sat down at the table and called her family.

After brief conversations with each of them and assurances that she would check in later, she hung up. Her next call was to Kevin. She hated bothering him on a Saturday morning, but this couldn't be helped.

"It's snowing here, too," he said after she updated him. "But nothing like where you are. What are your chances of getting here in time to go to work Monday?"

"From what the weather forecasters say, zero." The storm wasn't her fault. All the same, she felt guilty.

"When do you think you'll be back?"

"I wish I knew. This blizzard is supposed to last for days."

Kevin was silent a moment. "Make sure you get Carrie in line. Otherwise, she's toast."

"Believe me, I will." Gina wasn't about to explain to her boss that she hadn't spoken with her assistant in more than a week. She was ready to fire Carrie herself. "What do you want me to do about Evelyn Grant?"

"Bring in Lise."

Gina preferred to keep the account to herself, but she knew her friend would do a good job. "I'll call her today."

"You do that. Keep in touch."

As soon as Gina hung up, she dialed Carrie's cell number. After four rings, her assistant answered. "Hello?" she mumbled, sounding sleepy.

"I woke you," Gina said. "Are you still sick?"

"Not anymore. Hang on a sec."

Carrie covered the phone. Gina couldn't make out what her assistant said, but she definitely heard a man's voice.

"I'm back," Carrie said. "Did you get the email I sent yesterday?"

"I didn't get a chance to check." Tired as she'd been from her late night at the hospital, Gina hadn't even thought about email. "As of last night, we're in the middle of a blizzard. The airport is closed, and I could be stuck in Montana for days. I expect you to pull your weight at work. That means returning calls to any client who asks for me, and no more coming in late."

"All right." Carrie sounded sulky. "I just wish you'd read my email."

"What did it say?"

"I'd rather you read it."

Now Gina was seriously worried. "Thanks to this blizzard, it may be a while before I'm able to drive to a place where I can access Wi-Fi. You may as well tell me now."

Carrie hesitated and then let out a resigned breath. "Something amazing happened to me, Gina. I've fallen in love with Chad, and he's in love with me."

Gina wasn't sure what she'd expected, but it wasn't this. "But you barely know him," she said.

"I know him better than you think. When I came down with the flu last Sunday, he took care of me. We've been together every day and night since."

Six whole days. Gina suppressed a skeptical snort. "Great, but you can't just blow off our clients because you're in love with some guy you just met."

"Chad isn't just 'some guy,'" Carrie fired back, indignant. "He's the one—my soul mate. I had Thanksgiving dinner with his family, and he came to my parents' for dessert. They adore him, Gina. We're already talking about marriage and starting a family."

As incredulous as Gina was—who fell in love that quickly and stayed in love?—she almost envied her assistant. "Not just yet though, right?"

"No, but meeting Chad has changed everything. I realize now that a career in marketing isn't for me. I want a less stressful job, where I don't have to work such long hours or take my work home with me. That way, Chad and I can see more of each other."

Gina picked her jaw up off the floor. "But he works long hours, too," she said.

"That's true, but he enjoys what he does. I don't."

"You could've fooled me—you sure acted like you did."

"Because I thought I wanted to be like you. But I'm not you, and I need more in my life than just work."

Not sure whether to be flattered that Carrie had wanted to be like her or insulted that her assistant thought she had no life, Gina frowned. But Carrie was right. Without work, Gina had no life. Which was kind of pathetic but also necessary if she wanted to get ahead. "But you're on the fast track at Andersen, Coats and Mueller," Gina argued. "You want to move up in the company, don't you?"

"I thought I did, but I was wrong."

Wondering if the flu had addled Carrie's brain, Gina shook her head. "This job is the chance of a lifetime, Carrie. Don't throw away your future on an impulse. In a few days you're going to wake up, and I would hate for you to regret this."

"I don't think I will. The truth is, I've been thinking about switching jobs for over a month."

"You never said anything. You jumped at the opportunity to take care of my clients while I was gone and assured me that you could handle the responsibility. The day after I left, you worked so hard you fell asleep at your desk and didn't wake up until the next morning."

"That was awful."

"I'm sorry you had so much to do, but when I get back your workload will lighten up substantially. In the meantime, Evelyn Grant needs attention and so do our other clients. I'm counting on you, Carrie, to do what you promised and give the clients what they want and need."

"Yeah, okay. When did you say you'll be back?"

"As soon as the airport reopens. I'll keep you posted. I'm going to call Lise and ask her to step in and help with Grant Industries."

Her assistant sounded remarkably cheerful about that. So different from a week and a half ago.

Gina's temples began to throb, threatening a bear of a headache. After digging through her purse for the aspirin bottle and taking two tablets, she phoned Lise.

"Can you help me out?" she asked after explaining the situation.

"Kevin specifically asked for me to work with Evelyn Grant? That's so cool. I assume I'll also get part of the bonus from the account?"

Gina hated to give up a penny of that hard-earned money, but she didn't have much choice. "Absolutely. The hard-copy records are in my file cabinet." She gave Lise the password to access the information online.

"I've never experienced a blizzard," Lise said when the business part of the conversation ended. "What's it like?"

"Pretty, but a little scary." Especially with Zach still out there. Gina glanced anxiously at the window. "I just wish my uncle had installed Wi-Fi here."

"I don't blame you. If I had no internet and was stuck on a ranch in the middle of nowhere, I'd go nuts. How do you keep from losing your mind?"

If it wasn't for Zach, Gina knew she'd be pacing the house. "It isn't so bad," she said.

"Let me guess—you've met a sexy cowboy and he's keeping you company."

Her friend must be a mind reader. "Something like that."

"Mmm, that sounds intriguing."

The back door opened. With the wind howling at his back, Zach stomped his feet on the mat and stepped inside. Relief flooded her. His coat, gloves and face mask were coated in snow, but he was safe.

"I have to go," she told Lise. "I'll call you again soon."

"You better. I want the whole scoop on your cowboy."

By the time Gina disconnected, Zach had stripped off the face mask and gloves. His coat and boots followed.

"You made it back," Gina said.

"Thanks to the rope from the barn to the house. Visibility out there is near zero, and the snow is deep. Curly and I made half a dozen trips between the barn and west pasture to feed all the cattle."

"That sounds like a lot of work."

"Yep. I'm sure glad Pete fixed the water heater and the cattle have the water they need. Otherwise, we'd be in big trouble." Zach's stomach growled. "What's for breakfast?"

"How about a cheese omelet, bacon and toast? Sit down and I'll bring you a fresh cup of coffee while you wait."

Zach grinned. "I'm sure glad I won the game last night."

Gina put her hands on her hips. "Those are fighting words, Mr. Horton. Care for a repeat tonight?"

"Sure. Or we could try a different game. Lucky kept several on hand."

"Let's stick with Scrabble."

THE BLIZZARD CONTINUED throughout Monday and Tuesday with no signs of easing up. Zach and Curly spent hours feeding the cattle and checking the water supply and did what chores they could in the barn. Mostly they holed up in their respective shelters.

Avoiding the half-mile trek to the trailer and back every day was a relief, but staying in the same house as Gina was tough. Zach wanted her more every day, and keeping his hands to himself was torture.

He did his best to steer clear of her when he could, and they settled into a routine of sorts. Zach spent part of his day doing chores, and Gina continued to grapple with her job responsibilities and sort through Lucky's stuff. Zach helped her pack boxes destined for charity and fill bags with trash. Soon trash bags accumulated in the hallway, until there was hardly room to pass by.

Evenings, they took turns cooking dinner and then played various board games, with the loser making breakfast for the winner.

After dinner on Wednesday, the snow finally tapered off.

"Look at that." Gina pointed through the window on the kitchen door. "We can actually see the moon tonight."

Standing behind her, Zach inhaled her sweet scent. He was close enough that he could brush her hair aside, lean down and nuzzle her neck.

He stepped back and cleared his throat. "The roads should be cleared in a day or two."

"Just in the nick of time—the freezer is nearly empty. I wonder when the airport will reopen and when I can go home."

Soon, Zach hoped. He was enjoying Gina's company far too much and was tired of being in a constant state of arousal. He looked forward to going back to his trailer.

"Sometime this weekend, I'd guess," he said. "This is probably my last night in the house. We've played every board game here. What'll we do tonight?"

It was a loaded question because what he wanted was to fool around. But he'd promised to behave, and he would keep his word if it killed him. Which it just might.

Looking as if she'd read his mind, Gina swallowed and tugged the hem of her sweater over her hips. "They're showing one of my favorite movies on TV tonight. We could watch it."

"Which movie is that?"

*"It's a Wonderful Life."*

Zach remembered the film. "I haven't seen that since I was a kid. Sure. We'll make popcorn. Too bad we finished the remainder of the beer last night."

"We're out of wine, too. I could make hot chocolate."

"Then I really will feel like a kid again."

Gina checked her watch. "The movie starts in twenty minutes. I'll make the popcorn and cocoa right away."

"I'll light the fire."

By the time she brought in the refreshments, the fire was crackling and Zach had the TV turned to the right channel. He took the cocoa mugs from her and set them on the coffee table.

Gina wandered to the picture window and opened the

drapes. Moonlight lit the snow and stars glittered in the sky. "What a beautiful evening," she murmured.

And a beautiful woman staring into the night. Zach considered joining her at the window, but he didn't. Best to stay out of reach of temptation. "You don't see all those stars in Chicago," he said, taking his mug to the armchair. "Too much light pollution. If you lived here on the ranch—"

"Don't start that again." She sat down on the sofa. "You can't reach the popcorn all the way over there."

She had a point. Wary of sitting too close to her, he settled into one end of the sofa. Gina stayed at the opposite end. Now they both had to stretch to reach the popcorn.

The movie started. Zach watched for a while but soon got sidetracked by Gina. Looking intent and entranced, she leaned slightly toward the TV screen and silently mouthed much of the dialogue, right along with Donna Reid, Jimmy Stewart and the other actors.

During an ad, he muted the sound. "Just how many times have you seen this movie?"

"At least a dozen, maybe two."

"Seriously?"

"I told you, it's one of my favorites."

He chuckled and shook his head. "You're an *It's a Wonderful Life* junkie. I'd never have guessed."

"I love most every Christmas movie. I love Christmas, period."

Then why did she spend the holiday in Chicago year after year? Her work, Zach figured. She wanted to stay close by in case one of her clients needed her.

"You've been saying you want to spend more time with your family," he said. "Why don't you come back this year? You'd make them very happy."

"Because when I finally leave here, Christmas will

be less than two weeks away. It seems silly to fly home, then turn around and fly all the way back. Besides, I've already been here almost a week longer than I expected. I need to stay in Chicago, but I'll come back in the spring to tie up any loose ends at the house. Next year, I'll definitely be here for Christmas."

"Okay. Winter is a bad time to try to sell property around here. You may as well hold off on putting the Lucky A on the market until you come back next spring."

She kept insisting she was going to sell, but a few months down the road she might change her mind.

"You have a point, but I—" She broke off, snatched the remote from the coffee table and turned on the sound. "The movie's starting again."

Once again, she turned her attention to the TV screen.

Zach had trouble getting into the story, mainly because he couldn't concentrate on much besides Gina. He was too fixated on watching her lick her lips after she sipped her cocoa or swallowed a mouthful of popcorn. He couldn't help but imagine her tongue on him. With her every breath, her breasts rose and fell.

She was so damn sexy, and sitting a couple of arms' lengths from her ranked up there with the most difficult things he'd ever done. He seriously considered returning to the armchair, but he stayed where he was and fought a battle with his growing desire.

When Jimmy Stewart kissed Donna Reid for the first time, Gina glanced at him, her lips looking full and lush. "That's just about the most romantic kiss ever."

Her cheeks were flushed from the heat of the room and the tiny gold flecks in her eyes reflected the fire. She looked warm and inviting and irresistible.

But it was the longing on her face that did Zach in. She wanted him.

A certain part of his body began to rise. "We can top George Bailey and Mary Hatch anytime. But I made a promise not to kiss you, and I won't break it without your okay."

"Break it, Zach." She slid across the cushions, toward him.

He muted the TV and did what he'd been aching to do for days. Pulled her into his arms and kissed her.

She tasted of popcorn, cocoa and passion.

He'd missed this, wanted to go on kissing her, but after a few minutes, he reluctantly broke contact. "How does that compare to the kiss we just saw?"

"I'm not sure." She twined her hands around his neck. "Could we try it again?"

"I see no problem with that."

He kissed her again, and heat sizzled between them. That kiss blended into another and another. Zach forgot to think. Eager to touch her, he cupped her breasts.

With a pleased, purring sound she pushed her ample softness against his palms. He brushed his thumbs over her nipples and felt her shudder. His hands shook, he wanted her so badly.

He wanted more. A lot more. Somehow he managed to pull back. "This is dangerous," he said, breathing hard.

"Shhh." Gina pulled him down for another kiss.

He eased her back so that she lay against the sofa pillow. With her light brown hair spread across the pillow, her eyes closed and desire tinting her face and neck, she was beautiful. The most beautiful woman Zach had ever known.

He slipped his hands under her sweater and pushed it up so that he could see her. Her stomach was warm and smooth. She wore a lacy, white bra that plainly showed her dusky pink nipples, the points stiff against the lace.

Blood roared through his head. He unhooked the front clasp, pushed the bra aside and ran his tongue across one nipple.

Whimpering, Gina slid her restless hands under his shirt and up his back. Zach tasted the other breast. Her nails scraped lightly over his back.

His body was on fire, and his erection throbbed and demanded release. He was reaching for the button on her jeans when his elbow connected with the coffee table. It hurt like hell.

"Damn it."

"What happened?" Gina asked, looking slightly dazed.

"Bumped my funny bone." And a good thing he had. What was he doing?

He fastened her bra and tugged her sweater down.

"Are you okay?" Gina asked.

Her lips were lush and swollen from his kisses and her normally smooth hair was tangled and sexy. Zach wanted her more than he'd ever wanted a woman. But he wasn't right for Gina, and she wasn't right for him.

He was starting to care. Hell. He was so not okay.

He grabbed the remote. "Everything's fine."

She nodded and glanced at the TV screen. "We missed the end of the movie."

"That's okay. We know it has a happy ending."

At his sarcastic tone, she frowned. "You don't believe in happy endings?"

"Only in novels and movies." Zach flipped off the TV.

"That's sad."

He slanted her a look. "I'm a realist. How many couples with happy endings have you seen in real life?"

"I can think of several right here in Saddlers Prairie. Autumn and Cody Naylor, Jenny and Adam Dawson, Megan and Drew Dawson, Mark and Stacy Engle. Clay and Sarah—"

"Yeah, I get it. Some people do have happy endings."

But not Zach. He was alone, just as he wanted to be.

"You think I'm looking for a relationship with you," she said.

"Are you?"

"Of course not! I'm leaving in a few days." She tucked her hair behind her ears. "I'm not some naive girl, Zach. We kissed and you unfastened my bra. It was really nice, but that's all."

There was a lot more between them than that, and they both knew it.

And he needed space, needed to tamp his feelings down and keep them there. He stood. "I need to be up early. I'm going to turn in."

She nodded. "Who's making breakfast tomorrow?"

"I'll fix myself something before I leave. I'll be extra busy the next few days, clearing pathways around the ranch and catching up on chores I haven't been able to do. I probably won't see you again before you leave."

"Oh—okay." She glanced at her hands and then offered a bright smile. "Good night, Zach, and thank you for everything."

## Chapter Fourteen

By Friday the airport had reopened and the roads were finally clear enough to drive. Gina wanted to leave the next morning, but due to the blizzard and a glut of passengers, she couldn't get out until Sunday. As soon as she booked her ticket, she called her family.

"Hi," Gloria said.

"Good morning, cookie," Sophie chimed in from the extension phone. "I'll bet you're glad the roads are open."

"I am. I just got my ticket home. I leave Sunday morning. Let's have one last dinner together tomorrow night."

"That sounds lovely, but you don't want to cook on your last night in town."

"Actually, I've pretty much emptied the refrigerator," Gina said. Zach could take whatever was left. "I was thinking we could eat at Barb's Café." It was the only restaurant in town besides fast-food places. "My treat. Tell Uncle Redd to meet us at your house. I'll pick you up there and drive his car."

"You and Zach can sit in the front seat," Gloria said, her voice coy.

They all knew he'd stayed at the house during the blizzard. Gina wasn't about to feed their speculation frenzy. "Zach and I haven't seen each other in a few days." Not since the night of those melting kisses.

It was a relief not having to face him and having the house to herself again. At least that's what she told herself.

The truth was, she missed his company. She missed him.

Which was why she wanted to hurry back to Chicago and immerse herself in work.

"What do you mean, you haven't seen each other?" Sophie asked.

"I've been busy with my work and the house, and he's had a lot of ranching chores. I'm sure he's fine."

"After he stayed with you and made sure you were safe, that's all you have to say?"

"What do you expect me to say?"

Gloria snorted. "For a smart woman, you sure are thick sometimes. Zach cares about you."

"Of course he does. I'm Lucky's only niece. Now, what time should I pick you up?"

"Tell me you invited him to dinner."

"No, I didn't. This is a family dinner."

"And Zach is like family."

They were impossible. "You know what I mean," Gina said.

"I know what you *sound* like. You're avoiding him."

Which was true, but then, Zach was avoiding her, too. He seemed to think she wanted more from him than she did. Gina did have feelings for him, but she wasn't about to let them out. He wasn't the right guy for her. "Why would I do that?"

"I'm not in the mood for guessing games, Gina. What did you and Zach argue about?"

Would they never quit? "Oops, gotta run. See you tomorrow night."

Uncle Redd's line was busy when she tried to call him, so she called Carol Plett, the Realtor.

"This is the slowest time of year," Mrs. Plett said. "It's best to wait until January."

"Could you at least come look at it?" Gina asked. "I'm flying back to Chicago Sunday and would like to settle things before I leave."

"Unfortunately, I'm just about to leave for Elk Ridge to see my new little granddaughter. The blizzard kept me away from her last weekend, and I miss her. I've been in Lucky's house many times and I know the ranch well. I'll draw up the listing papers and send them to you."

When Gina hung up, she tried Uncle Redd again. This time, she reached him. "Meet us at Gloria and Sophie's at five-thirty," she said after inviting him to dinner.

"It's a date. Gloria says you and Zach had a fight."

Her cousin hadn't wasted any time passing on her suspicions. "That's not true," Gina said. "What's wrong with wanting a meal alone with my family? Hey, will you drive me to the airport Sunday morning? My plane leaves at eight, and we'd have to leave around five-thirty."

"At that hour it's still dark out, and you don't want me driving all that way in the dark. Besides, I don't get up as early as I used to. Why don't you ask Zach—since you two aren't in a fight? He gets up early, so he won't mind."

Gina was sure he would. If only she could call a cab. Unfortunately there were none in Saddlers Prairie. She thought about asking Autumn or one of the other women she knew for a ride, but they all had families and she didn't want to impose.

She sighed. "I don't have much choice, do I?"

DESPITE HAVING BEEN plowed, Saturday night the roads were coated with black ice. Returning from dinner at Barb's, Gina piloted Uncle Redd's sedan at well below the speed limit.

In the passenger seat, Sophie smiled. "Tonight was wonderful fun—and so yummy. I've always enjoyed the food at Barb's."

"Home cooked is better, though," Gloria said from the backseat.

Sophie sniffed. "I know that, Gloria, but eating out is about more than just the food. It's nice to be waited on and let someone else cook. Best of all, there are no dishes."

"And Sugar and Bit get the bones—a real treat for them," Uncle Redd added. He was sharing the back with Gloria.

After working on the house all day and carting a truckload of donations to the school and church, Gina had needed to get out and had enjoyed the evening with her family—bickering and all. "You know you could eat there every week, if you wanted," she said.

"Waste all that money?" Uncle Redd snorted.

Sophie nodded. "He's right. We don't have the kind of income you do, cookie. Living on Social Security and a small pension doesn't leave much for extras."

"Sophie!" Gloria scolded. "We may not have Gina's business smarts and financial resources, but we're comfortable, and you know it. Thank you for treating us, Gina."

"Yes—thank you, cookie."

Gina would've died if they'd realized how broke she was. She smiled. "It was my pleasure."

Gloria leaned up and touched her shoulder. "We're really going to miss you."

Uncle Redd and Sophie murmured agreement.

"I'll miss you, too," Gina said. Along with everyone else in Saddlers Prairie—her friends and, most of all, Zach.

"I wish you'd come back for Christmas," Uncle Redd said.

Lise had invited Gina over for brunch again, which was

something to look forward to, but the rest of the day was bound to be lonely. "I've already been here for nearly a week longer than I planned," she explained. "I can't afford to take any more time away. But I'll be back in the spring, and I promise I'll be here for Christmas next year."

With any luck, by then the Lucky A would be sold. Her heart wrenched at the thought, and not just because there would be no more Christmases there.

She was beginning to think she should keep it. Which was ridiculous. The ranch would never be profitable, not without a large infusion of cash she didn't have. She needed to sell and would put it on the market in January.

"Someone ought to live in that house and take care of it until it sells," Uncle Redd said. "Zach should move in."

Gina hadn't thought of that, but it was a good idea.

A block before she reached Gloria and Sophie's house, she slowed down. "It's slippery out there. I'm going to walk you two inside. Uncle Redd, you can wait in the car."

Gloria waved off the suggestion. "Nonsense. Why, only a few hours ago Zach came by and cleared and salted our walk—just as he promised he would before the blizzard. I wasn't going to tell you this because you said you didn't want him to come tonight, but I invited him anyway, as a way of thanking him for all that he does. He couldn't make it."

Gina was relieved about that. She wasn't great at pretending to be relaxed and happy when she wasn't. If Zach had come tonight, fooling her family wouldn't have been easy. It was bad enough that she would see him tomorrow.

"For the last time, we're not fighting—he's taking me to the airport in the morning, remember? I'll ask him about moving into the house then." As soon as he dropped her off and drove away, she would push him from her thoughts—and her heart. "Tonight I wanted to have dinner with just us," she added.

"Well, I missed him," Sophie said. Gina pulled to a stop in front of the house. "What time is your flight?"

"Eight a.m. We'll leave the ranch at five-thirty."

Gloria opened her door. "Wait for me," Gina ordered. Taking care not to slip, she headed around the car.

"I don't need any help." Gloria's mouth tightened, but she allowed Gina to take her arm. "Have a safe trip home, and call to let us know you made it."

"No matter what time you get in," Sophie added, grasping hold of Gina's other arm.

As they made their way slowly toward their front door, Gloria shook her off. "The walkway is just fine, Gina. I'm not a doddering fool. I'm quite capable of—"

Her words died as she lost her footing and slipped. Gina grabbed for her, but it was too late. Her cousin fell hard on the walkway.

Gina covered her mouth with her hands. "Are you okay?"

"I skinned my palm and twisted my ankle, but I'm all right."

As Gina extended her arms to help her cousin to her feet, Uncle Redd exited the car. "Let me give you a hand," he called out.

The last thing Gina needed was for him to slip and fall, too. "It's okay," she called out. "Please wait in the car."

"I'm fine," Gloria insisted.

Pulling a two-hundred-pound woman to her feet was no easy task, and Gina grunted with the effort. Gloria leaned heavily on her and limped slowly forward.

Gina frowned. "You're in pain."

"I'll live."

"Maybe we should call Dr. Mark," Sophia suggested, looking worried.

"I'm not going to bother the poor doctor on a Saturday night. I'll clean my palm, ice the ankle and take two aspirin, and everything will be fine. Go on now, Gina. Drive Redd home and drive yourself back to the house so you can get a decent night's sleep."

"You're sure?" Gina asked as Sophie opened the front door. "Let me come in and take a look at your ankle."

"You're not a doctor, and I don't need a nursemaid."

Her cousin set her jaw and Gina knew that arguing was pointless. "Okay." She hugged both her cousins. "I'll miss you both so much."

"Us, too, cookie," Sophie said. "Don't forget to call when you get home."

ANTSY TO LEAVE, Gina was up and dressed early Sunday morning. As she sipped coffee and waited for Zach, she glanced around the kitchen. Without the clutter, it looked bigger. A couple of coats of paint and some new curtains would do wonders for it.

Would she be able to stay there this spring, or would new owners already be living in the house?

Saying goodbye to the place where she'd spent many happy weeks every summer of her childhood made her heart ache, and she half wished she could stay. Which was ridiculous. Her life was in Chicago, and she could hardly wait to get back to work. Back to the comforts of her own apartment. Wi-Fi, a great music system and a flat-screen TV. Entertainment and good restaurants within walking distance. She filled a Thermos with the coffee she'd made and washed out the pot. And really good coffee.

Footsteps thudded on the back stoop, followed by a knock. Zach.

He was freshly shaved, wide-awake and so handsome that her heart lifted at the sight of him.

"Morning," he said in a gruff voice, sounding as if they were his first words of the day. He wiped his feet on the welcome mat and stepped inside. "Ready to go?"

"Almost. I want to ask you something."

That earned her a wary look.

"Don't worry, I wouldn't dream of prying into your past."

His eyes narrowed a fraction. He didn't like that. She hurried on. "I was talking with my family last night, and we think that you should move into the house until it sells. It's not good for it to be empty." But it was more than that. For reasons she couldn't define, she needed Zach to stay here.

"I cleaned out most of Uncle Lucky's junk and the fridge is empty," she went on, "but the towels, linens and kitchen things are still here."

She sucked in a breath and waited.

"Sure, I'll stay here."

Overcome with relief, she exhaled. "That's great."

Her gaze collided with his. The warmth she saw there confused her and made her want to cry. Uncomfortable, she held out the Thermos. "This is for you to drink on the way to the airport."

"I could use more coffee. Why don't you hold on to it while I load your bags into the truck?"

When the last suitcase disappeared from the kitchen, Gina shut off the light. She thought about locking the door, but as far as she knew, Uncle Lucky had never locked up. She left it as he would have. It was still dark outside, and now the house was dark, too.

After buckling up, she handed Zach the keys to the house.

He pocketed them and pulled out of the driveway. "I'm ready for some of that coffee now."

"Sure." Gina opened the Thermos and filled the cup.

He was quiet for a while, sipping and keeping his eyes on the deserted highway.

Tension filled the truck, not much different from the night they'd met. But so much had happened since then. She couldn't leave things like that.

"Zach, I—"

"I don't want—"

They spoke at the same time.

"Go ahead," Zach said.

"You first."

He nodded. "I left a little abruptly the other night. I… It wasn't anything you did. I enjoyed being with you—all of it."

His eyes were warm again, and she all but melted. "Me, too."

The next stretch of silence was far more relaxed.

"Shoot," she said. "I left the hat you loaned me in the house. It's in the coat closet."

"Okay. How was the dinner with your family last night?" he asked.

"Fine, until the end of the evening. I was helping Gloria up the walk, but you know how independent she is. She shrugged me off and, of course, slipped on black ice. She twisted her ankle. I was able to get her inside, but she wouldn't let me examine her ankle. She promised to take a couple of aspirin and ice it. I think she'll be okay."

"She's tough. What's on your agenda when you get back?"

"If my flights are on time—please, God—and I get home at a decent hour, I'll probably stop at the office and get ready for Monday. I'll be touching bases with all my clients and visiting a few in person." Starting with Evelyn Grant. If she'd even see her. Gina had spoken with Lise several times. She and Ms. Grant seemed to be getting along well, but Gina wanted the woman to give her another chance.

"I'll bet the people you work with will be glad to see you back."

"I'll be glad to see them, too." Except for Carrie. According to Marsha, she'd been coming to work on time but leaving at five o'clock sharp. Employees at Andersen, Coats and Mueller rarely left at five, and it was obvious that her heart was no longer in the job. Either she was going to quit, or Gina would have to let her go.

"I've been wondering, Zach. When the ranch sells, where will you go?"

"Maybe you'll keep it and I won't have to go anywhere."

"Very funny. I can't keep it. How many times do I have to tell you that?"

"Hey, I'm just doing what I promised Lucky I'd do."

She couldn't help admiring him for his persistence. "You should've been in sales," she teased. "You're great at refusing to take 'no' for an answer."

"But not so hot at closing the deal."

"Not this deal. So what are your plans for after the ranch sells?"

"Haven't thought much about that yet."

Of course he hadn't. Which just underlined how different he was from Gina.

Suddenly her cell phone rang. Before 6:00 a.m.? She pulled it from her purse and glanced at the screen. What she saw worried her.

"It's a call from Flagg Memorial Hospital." She bit her lip. "Don't tell me Redd had another attack of indigestion.

He needs to get that physical." Zach shot her a worried look before she answered. "Hello?"

"It's Sophie."

"Hi, Sophie. What are you doing at the hospital?" Gina asked. "Before you answer that, I'm putting you on speaker so Zach can hear."

"Hi, Zach."

"Hey, Sophie."

"We missed you at dinner last night. In case Gina didn't tell you, Gloria slipped on black ice and twisted her ankle on our own walk. She skinned her hand pretty bad, too, trying to break the fall. It's not your fault, though. You did a fine job clearing off the snow and ice. I guess Gloria found a patch you missed."

"But she swore she was all right," Gina said. The sun wasn't close to rising, and outside it was still pitch-black. She frowned. "You shouldn't drive in the dark, Sophie, especially on the slippery roads. Why didn't you call and let me come get you?"

"Because you have a long travel day ahead of you, and you needed your rest. But don't worry, cookie, I wasn't about to drive. I called Uncle Redd instead."

"He isn't supposed to drive in the dark, either," Gina said. "That's why Zach is driving me to the airport instead of Uncle Redd." She realized that her uncle was just as invested in her getting together with Zach as her cousins.

Zach shook his head. "Tell us what's going on, Sophie."

"Gloria's hand is pretty banged up, and X-rays showed that her ankle is broken. They're keeping her in the hospital for a few more hours. She's sleeping right now, which is a blessing, if only because she's stopped complaining."

Despite the seriousness of the situation, Zach's lips quirked. Gina couldn't stifle her smile, either.

"When we get her home, she's supposed to stay off

her foot and rest her hand for a few days," Sophie went on. "Can you imagine? Gloria hates for other people to take care of her."

"No kidding," Gina muttered.

"The nurse says she'll need crutches, but with her poor hand, how is she supposed to use them?" Sophie sighed. "I just wish we had an extra bedroom downstairs so she could sleep on the main floor. Hold on." She covered the phone for a moment and then returned. "I have to go— someone else needs to use the phone."

"Call us back," Gina said, wishing her cousin owned a cell phone.

"If I can. Have a safe flight."

"Bummer," Zach said when Gina disconnected.

"Oh, man, a broken ankle. I could've taken Gloria to the hospital last night, only she insisted she was fine. I don't see how Sophie will be able to take care of her."

"She's an Arnett, and Arnetts always manage," Zach said. "That's what Lucky used to say."

Manage or not, Gina couldn't leave her family, not like this. Praying that Kevin would understand, she glanced at Zach. "Please take me to the hospital."

## Chapter Fifteen

Zach was more than a little surprised by Gina's request to go to the hospital. Just as he was starting to relax. Keeping his distance the past few days hadn't been easy, and knowing he was taking her to the airport and wouldn't see her again for several months had been a big relief.

But now… "Are you sure?" he asked. "Your flight leaves in ninety minutes."

"I wasn't around for Uncle Lucky. I'm not going to make that same mistake again. I'll have to fly out later."

He gave her a sideways look. "Will your boss be okay with that?"

"He'll have to be."

Zach wasn't okay. He understood about Gloria, but he wanted Gina far away, out of temptation's reach.

Thirty minutes later, he and Gina were headed down the hospital hall toward Gloria's room. Even before they reached the room, he heard Gloria's querulous voice. "I want to go home."

"You know we have to wait for the doctor to discharge you," Redd replied.

"That's right," Sophie said. "Be patient."

"Don't you boss me around, little sister."

Gina rolled her eyes at Zach. "They don't sound any different than they always do."

Pasting a smile on her face, she entered the room. "Hi, Gloria." She bent over the hospital bed and kissed her cousin's cheek.

Not wanting to interfere, Zach hung back.

Instead of seeming glad to see her niece, the older woman glanced from Gina to Zach and frowned. "What are you two doing here? You should be on your way to the airport."

"I've decided to stay for a few more days," Gina said. "Until I know you're okay."

Sophie looked relieved, but Gloria's lips tightened. "Of course, I'm okay. It's not like I'm dying. How are you, Zach? We missed you at dinner last night."

"So your sister said. How's that ankle?"

"I'm on pain meds and I feel pretty good. I just wish people would stop fussing over me." Gloria wore a stubborn look that reminded Zach of Gina. "I want to go home."

Her younger sister let out a fed-up sigh. "Yes, you keep telling us that. You—"

Redd quickly cut in. "Once we leave, we have a bit of a problem. Glo needs crutches, but with her sore hand she'll only be able to use one."

"I'm afraid that's true," Gloria admitted. "But I'll make it work."

Zach had his doubts. She wouldn't be able to get around easily. As independent as she was, she wasn't going to like that.

Suddenly Gina's stomach grumbled.

Gloria raised her eyebrows. "Skipped breakfast, did you? You better head on down to the cafeteria and get yourself something to eat."

"But I just got here," Gina said. "I don't want to leave you, except maybe to talk to the doctor."

"There'll be time for that after you've eaten. You must be hungry, too, Zach. Both of you—go. And bring us back something. Hospital food is dismal, and we're all running on empty."

"What would you like?" Zach asked.

"A cinnamon roll or doughnuts would be nice." Sophie looked hopeful.

"Not for me." Redd rubbed his chest, as if remembering his bad case of indigestion. "I better stick with a bagel and jam."

"That reminds me," Gina said. "You need to schedule a physical."

Moments later, Zach and Gina entered the empty elevator. He smelled her perfume. His body stirred and he wished to hell that Gloria had never slipped and that Gina was on a plane that would take her away.

"Gloria seems in decent spirits," he said.

"As argumentative as ever. This isn't going to be fun for her—or any of us." She tapped her finger against her lip. "Gloria needs a place to sleep where she doesn't have to climb the stairs. I'm thinking she should stay at the ranch and sleep in the downstairs bedroom."

"Good plan—if you can convince her. I'm happy to continue staying in my trailer." Which would help him keep his distance. If he had to see Gina, he would make sure he wasn't alone with her.

The elevator dinged and opened its doors on the lower level and they stepped off.

"I'm going to call my boss now," Gina said. "I'll meet you in the cafeteria."

Zach was selecting a variety of bagels and sweet breakfast treats when she joined him.

"Did you talk to your boss?" he asked.

"He didn't answer, so I left a message. That's a lot of food."

"We're a bunch of hungry people."

"We better get back upstairs and feed my cousins before they bicker to death."

"PLEASE GIVE ME the remote," Gloria said. It seemed to be her umpteenth demand since Gina had helped her to the living room sofa. "Then I want some tea. I have tea bags in my purse."

Gina handed her cousin the remote. "I'll go heat up the water and add tea to the grocery list."

She headed for the kitchen, wishing her family would hurry back. Zach had taken Sophie to get her car and pack some of Gloria's belongings. Uncle Redd had gone home to feed Sugar and Bit.

Gina microwaved a mug of water. She brought the mug, a tea bag from her cousin's purse and a bowl of sugar to the living room. Busy channel surfing, Gloria took one sip and then yawned and set the mug down. "I think I'll take a nap."

"But what about your tea?"

"I'll drink it later."

Gina nodded. "I'll get you a blanket." When she returned with a quilt, Gloria was snoring away, her foot propped on a pillow on the coffee table.

After tucking the cover around her, Gina tiptoed out. She needed to drive to Spenser's and stock up on groceries, but she wasn't about to leave Gloria alone.

She was sitting at the kitchen table, making a grocery list, when her cell phone rang. It was Kevin.

Before answering, she closed the door between the kitchen and hallway.

"That's too bad about your cousin, but we need you at the office," Kevin said after she explained the situation.

"I know, and I really want to be there, but this can't be helped. She's in a lot of pain and her sister can't care for her by herself."

"There are nurses and licensed caretakers for that sort of thing."

True, but if Gina so much as mentioned hiring someone to take care of Gloria, her cousin would have a fit. "For now, it's best that I'm here," she said. "Just give me a few more days."

"You said the same thing when you were stuck in the blizzard. That was bad enough, but there was nothing you could do about it and I understood. But this... I don't understand. If it was something life threatening, sure, but it's a broken ankle." Kevin made a disapproving sound.

Gina wasn't about to explain that she felt guilty for neglecting her relatives. "She's family, Kevin, and she's old. She needs me."

"Your clients need you, too. Maybe you've forgotten them."

"I've worked for you for nearly seven years. You know I'm not like that. I'll call them in the morning and explain, and I'll be back as soon as I possibly can. It won't be long, I promise."

"This elderly relative of yours isn't going to heal quickly. You could be gone weeks."

Gina hoped not, but unfortunately, Kevin was likely right.

She was silent a moment too long. He harrumphed. "You need to get your priorities straight."

"Work is my priority, just as it always has been."

"I'm beginning to doubt that. Christmas is only two

and a half weeks away. You stay in Montana and use the time to think about what you really want."

"But—"

"I've always liked you, Gina, but I don't think you fit at Andersen, Coats and Mueller anymore."

"You're firing me?" Her heart nearly stopped. "But I'm on track to be your next vice president."

"Things change. Lise has been handling Grant Industries quite well, and Evelyn requested that she take over the account. I was going to talk to you about that tomorrow, but you're not coming in. I'll parcel out the rest of your accounts to our other associates."

Gina swallowed around her suddenly dry throat. "But I'm sure that if I talk to Carrie, she'll—"

"We both know that Carrie isn't working out. Since you won't be here to fire her, I will."

"I understand." She bit her lip. "What about my year-end bonus?"

She needed that money to pay her current bills.

"You'll get your salary through the end of the year, and you can cash out any vacation time you haven't taken. I don't think you've earned your bonus."

She couldn't bear to think of what would happen without it. Creditors would hound her to death. She might even go bankrupt. Humiliation for what could be made her feel sick. She refused to be like her parents.

"I'm not just talking about Grant Industries," she argued, emboldened out of desperation. "I brought in several new clients this year and earned quite a bit of money for the company. I deserve to be compensated."

"You almost cost me the Grant account. No bonus, Gina, but if you want to come back, you can take Carrie's job." Kevin disconnected.

In shock, she gaped at the phone. Kevin had never

been the most compassionate man. His main interest had always been the bottom line. How many employees had come and gone because they fell short of his expectations? Gina had always produced. She'd prided herself on earning his trust and had never imagined she would one day join their ranks.

After putting in all those years of hard work and loyalty, it hurt. Now what was she supposed to do, and what would she tell her family and friends here in Saddlers Prairie? They all thought she was a rich and successful marketing professional, and she couldn't bear to lose their respect.

What to do, what to do? Her mind working furiously, she prowled around the kitchen. Finally she came up with something. She would explain that she'd decided to stay through December so that she could take care of Gloria and spend Christmas with her family.

Footsteps thudded across the back stoop, and she barely had a moment to compose herself. Sophie, Uncle Redd and the two dogs crowded through the door.

And, oh, dear God, Zach. Why did he have to be here now, when Kevin's words had barely sunk in? More than anyone else, Gina couldn't bear for him to know the truth. She wasn't sure why she needed him to believe she was successful, but she did.

Forcing a cheerful expression, she held a finger to her lips and kept her voice low. "Gloria's asleep in the living room."

Avoiding Zach's gaze, she bent to pet the dogs as they licked her face.

"Gina?" Zach said.

He sounded concerned. Realizing she was frowning, she quickly smoothed her expression. "Yes?"

"Where do you want me to put these suitcases?"

"Just leave them in here. When Gloria wakes up, I'll move them."

"One of those is mine," Sophie said. "I don't like staying alone in that house."

With Sophie here, too, Gina would have to pretend she was happy all the time. Wonderful. "That's fine," she said brightly. "There's certainly room for you. What about you, Uncle Redd?"

Her uncle shook his head. "I'd rather sleep in my own bed. But the dogs and I will stay for dinner tonight."

"Will you join us, Zach?" Sophie asked.

"Sorry, I can't."

That was a relief—she wouldn't have to pretend quite so hard at dinner. "Now that you're here to keep an eye on Gloria, I'm going to drive to Spenser's and pick up some groceries," she said.

"I'll follow you out." Zach shot her a questioning look and reached for the doorknob.

He was going to ask her what was wrong. Great, just great. Gina shrugged into her coat and grabbed her purse. In an effort to forestall any questions, she turned toward her cousin and uncle. "You should all know that while you were gone, I talked with my boss. I've decided to stay here through the holidays."

Redd grinned, and Sugar and Bit wagged their tails and yipped with excitement.

"That's wonderful, cookie." Sophie laid her palm over her heart. "I know your uncle Lucky is smiling down at you. He'll be downright euphoric when you put up the Christmas lights and a tree."

SOMETHING WAS WRONG. Zach couldn't put his finger on exactly what, but Gina looked shell-shocked.

"Are you sure you want to be here for three more weeks?" he asked as he shut the back door behind them.

"This way, I'll be able to spend Christmas with the family and do a few more things at the house before the Realtor lists the property."

"Your boss is okay with that?"

Instead of meeting his gaze, she pulled the key to Lucky's truck from her purse. "I decided to use up some of my vacation time."

"But this won't really be a vacation. You'll still be working with your clients."

She seemed to find the keys fascinating. "I'm going to let people at the office handle my clients."

She was a workaholic, she wouldn't meet his gaze and nothing she said made sense. Zach gave her a sideways look. "Tell me you're not doing this out of guilt."

"Partly. Look, I don't want to be away from Gloria for long—I better get going."

She left him scratching his head, wondering what was really going on.

# Chapter Sixteen

Zach was heading out to pick up a few things Curly needed to repair the tractor motor when he spotted Gina—climbing a ladder. For the past few days he'd mostly avoided her, only stopping by the house to briefly visit with Gloria and Sophia. Knowing she was within easy reach and would be for the next few weeks was killing him. Just as it had before.

He couldn't avoid her now. Wearing the same navy cap he'd loaned her weeks ago and her burgundy jacket, she was making her way up with strands of Christmas lights looped over one shoulder. Was she nuts?

He braked to a stop, strode straight to the ladder and gripped the base.

"Do you know how dangerous this is?" he said. "The ground is icy. The ladder legs could slip and you could fall."

"I'm being very careful," she replied. "I made sure to pack the snow around the—"

The lights fell from her shoulder and sailed down, barely missing his head, and the ladder jerked to the side. If he hadn't been here to grab on to it, Gina would've tumbled twenty feet down.

He shuddered to think of that.

"You climb down *now*," he ordered, the close call making him sound brusque.

The second her feet touched the ground, Zach pulled her around and gripped her shoulders. His hands shook a little. "Don't you ever do anything that crazy again!"

In the weak winter sun, her widened eyes looked especially green and reflected his own fear. She swallowed. "I'm sorry. I don't know what got into me. Trying to do everything myself, I guess."

"You and your aunt Gloria," he muttered. "Next time, ask for help."

He wanted to both shake her and kiss her until they forgot her near accident. But that would be as reckless as her solo climb up the ladder. Besides, her nosy cousins were peering out the kitchen window.

He let her go and then scooped the lights from the snowy ground. "I'll put these up. You hold the ladder."

Gina didn't argue.

By the time he finished he was calm again. "Let's see if they work. Go ahead and turn them on."

Moments later, twinkling lights outlined the roof of the house.

"They look so pretty," Gina said. "And to think that I only decided to put them up to get out of the house for a while."

"Let me take a wild guess—your cousins are getting on your nerves."

"Ya think? They went at each other nonstop while I put up the tree this morning and I really needed a break. I've run out of errands that will get me out of here, and I've visited my friends so often that their kids are beginning to think I'm family."

"Is Gloria feeling any better today?"

"A little. She's determined to use the crutches despite

her sore hand. She's anxious to go back to her own house, but I can't see her getting up and down the stairs for a while yet. It sure would be nice to have the house to myself. Between Gloria's demands and complaints, Sophie's nonstop chatter and their constant bickering, I'm about to lose my mind."

Zach could just imagine. He glanced at them through the window, and they smiled and waved.

Gina followed his gaze and frowned. "Did you see that? Gloria just threw us a thumbs-up. I think she's pleased to see us talking. The way she, Sophie and Uncle Redd keep singing your praises, it's obvious what they want. Oh, brother."

"They never have been subtle."

Even though her cousins were out of hearing range, Gina lowered her voice. "If you can think of anything else to get me out of the house, let me know."

Zach had some interesting ideas, but what he wanted was off-limits. "Maybe you should talk to your boss about working from here after all, and save your vacation days for something fun."

She all but recoiled. "I don't think I'll do that."

She didn't offer an explanation and Zach wasn't about to press her for one. As curious as he was, how she spent her time here was none of his business.

He shrugged. "If you want, you can give me a hand with some of the chores." Not that he needed help this time of year.

"Sure. What do you have in mind?"

"Bert just let the horses out to pasture. Their stalls need mucking out, and someone needs to bring them in again and brush and feed them."

Cleaning stalls was no fun, and he expected her to

turn down the offer. Instead she jumped on it. "I used to muck out the stalls for Uncle Lucky. I'll do it right now."

"Seriously? You must be desperate."

She shot a quick look at the kitchen window and winced. "More than you'd ever guess."

GINA'S IDENTITY HAD been tied up in her job for so long. Without clients and projects to fill the days, she felt purposeless and restless, like a ship adrift at sea. She was also worried sick about her finances.

Caring for the horses was a godsend. The gentle animals didn't judge her, and their blatant bids for attention made her laugh and took her out of herself. She'd convinced Zach and the other ranch hands to let her take care of them every day.

Often someone else was in the barn, mending harnesses, oiling saddles or loading the flatbed with hay for the cattle. Zach was always with one or more of his men, and she never saw him alone.

He was friendly but distant, which was safer for Gina. It was better that way. But she missed his warmth and their conversations.

Nine days after Gloria's accident, on a cold, clear afternoon, Gina was standing on a rung of the wood corral fence, fretting about money and watching the horses frisk about, when Zach joined her.

"Need help bringing in the horses?" he asked, stepping up next to her.

She shook her head. "They're having such a good time that I decided to leave them out a while longer. They're fun to watch."

A few of the animals nickered and started toward Zach. He grinned. "They can be real hams."

Gina nodded at Lightning. "Do you think he misses Uncle Lucky?"

"Sure he does, but he seems to like you."

"He likes you more." The horse all but ignored her in favor of Zach. "They all do."

"They know I have treats." He pulled a baggie of sliced apples from his pocket. "Take some."

Gina placed an apple slice in her palm, held out her arm and clicked her tongue. "Come here, Lightning." The horse gently took the apple from her and chuffed his thanks.

"Do that every day, and he'll love you forever," Zach said.

She didn't remind him that she wasn't going to be here forever.

When the apples were gone, he stepped down, his boots crunching on the hard snow. "Let's bring them in now."

Gina opened the gate and the horses trotted toward the barn.

Compared to the frigid air outside, the barn felt warm. The smells of hay, horses and leather reminded her of her childhood and filled her with nostalgia for those days. Days she'd gladly left behind years ago—or so she'd thought. Now she actually enjoyed being here.

When had that happened?

Zach helped her brush the horses. While they worked, he seemed at ease, and they talked as they had before the tension between them had become like a wall.

"I need your help," she said as they hung up the brushes.

"Don't tell me—you want to string lights around the barn roof." Zach's lips twitched, and for the first time in days, she laughed.

"No, but this *is* about Christmas. There are only nine

shopping days left, and I don't have any idea what to get Redd, Gloria or Sophie."

"Being here is enough."

"Besides that. I'd like to give them each something they really want." Nothing too pricey. Gina really had to watch her spending now. "I'm planning to drive to Elk Ridge tomorrow to go shopping, and I'm open to ideas." The town had a mall with several decent stores.

Zach didn't even hesitate. "I know something that doesn't require driving or shopping. Keep the Lucky A."

The longer Gina was here, the less she wanted to sell. But with her money troubles, she couldn't even entertain the thought of holding on to the ranch. She needed the proceeds to pay down her debt. "I'm putting it on the market in January—you know that."

"Then Elk Ridge, it is. I happen to be heading there in the morning to pick up a part for the tractor. Let's carpool."

She could easily take Uncle Lucky's truck, but the way it guzzled gas... "Okay, but I have no idea what I'm shopping for, and I could be a while."

"No problem—I need to pick up gifts for my family, too. We'll leave right after the morning chores and get an early start."

At the door of the barn, Zach plucked something from the hat he now considered hers. "Straw."

"Why does that not surprise me? I probably stink like the stalls."

He leaned in and sniffed. "I smell horse and hay but mostly flowers. I like that perfume."

"It's very high-end stuff called eau de shampoo."

They both smiled. He glanced at her mouth and sobered. Gina recognized that intense look. He was going to kiss her.

Although her mind warned her that that was dangerous, every cell in her body strained toward him.

Zach cupped her face between his roughened hands and kissed her, and she felt as if she'd finally come home. Grasping his shoulders, she leaned into his solid body.

One kiss wasn't enough and neither of them pulled away. All the passion and feeling Gina had stuffed down deep inside bubbled up.

Sometime later, breathing hard, Zach rested his forehead against hers. "You don't taste like horses, either."

"That's a relief."

His silvery eyes shone with feeling. A warm glow started in her heart and spread through her. She wanted Zach, but what she felt was so much more than desire.

She was falling in love with him.

That scared her. She knew what she wanted—a meaningful career, a life free of financial struggle and a man who was as driven to succeed as she was. Zach wasn't that man.

There was only one solution—to fall out of love with him.

Oh, that wouldn't be easy. Impossible, as long as she was there and seeing him all the time. She may as well enjoy what time she had left with him. When she got back to Chicago, she'd lick her wounds, find a new job and move on.

She made a show of glancing at her watch. "I better go inside and make sure Gloria and Sophie haven't murdered each other."

Zach opened the barn door and gestured her out. "I'll see you in the morning."

ZACH HATED CHRISTMAS shopping and usually did most of it online. But after picking up the tractor part, he decided to join the hordes of frenzied shoppers at the mall. After depositing the gifts he'd bought for the Arnetts in his truck, he sat down in the crowded food court to wait for Gina.

Gina. She was never out of his thoughts. He hadn't meant to kiss her yesterday, had fully intended to stick to his self-imposed distance. But she'd looked into his eyes with so much feeling and yearning that he hadn't been able to stop himself.

The passion in her kisses had nearly knocked him to his knees and erased his already shaky resolve to stay away from her. He no longer cared that acting on his desire was dangerous. His every waking thought was of making love with her. Soon.

Spotting her across the way, he waved. A smile bloomed on her face, and she strode toward him.

"Success!" she said, setting her bags down and sliding into a chair across the table.

Her cheeks were pink with excitement and her eyes sparkled.

Drawn into her web of happiness, Zach grinned like a love-struck fool. "I found what I needed, too," he said. "How about a quick bite before we head back to the ranch? I'm running on empty."

Gina laughed. "Of course you are."

While they dined on mall fare, he asked Gina what she got her family.

"Uh-uh." She shook her head. "You'll have to wait until Christmas morning. Show me what you got yours."

"Can't—I had them sent. I bought a Nerf basketball set for my nephew and a Play-Doh kit for my niece."

"They'll love those."

"That's what the clerk who sold them to me said." He shrugged. "They get so much stuff they probably won't even notice."

"Of course they will—you're their uncle. What did you get your dad and stepmom?"

"The usual—a fruit basket. I always get my mother perfume and I give my brother and his wife gourmet chocolate."

Gina didn't comment. She didn't have to—her frown spoke volumes. He shrugged. "Hey, at least they won't return that stuff."

"Ah, they must be difficult to please."

"In every way. My father thinks I'm wasting my life."

Now why had he told Gina what he hadn't even shared with Lucky? She angled her head, curious. Ready to rebuff any questions, he sucked in a breath.

She surprised him and said nothing. That was good. Real good, but instead of feeling relieved, he wanted to tell her about the mistake that had changed his life.

Which gave him pause. He didn't talk about that.

Besides, right now she seemed relaxed and happy, and he didn't want to ruin her mood. Deep down, he suspected she might side with his family, believing he'd done nothing wrong and that he was out of his mind for giving up his old life. Zach couldn't handle that kind of condemnation, not from her.

He stacked their plates and stood to carry them to the trash. "It'll be dark soon. We should head back or your family will start to worry."

"They won't worry. They'll speculate, wondering what we're doing together."

Her laughter brought a smile to his face. Once again, he relaxed. By the time he pulled onto the highway, the sun had set.

Gina settled back in her seat. "Thanks for this. I really needed to get away for the day."

"No problem."

"Are you going to the Christmas party at the Dawson Ranch Friday night?" she asked.

"I go every year."

"Good, then you can help with Gloria. She'll have a fit if she misses it. What's it like?"

"Noisy and crowded, but fun. Everyone in town is there."

Neither of them spoke again. The warmth and darkness of the truck felt private and intimate. As Zach steered the truck toward home, he realized that he wasn't ready to go to the ranch just yet. A few miles from the Lucky A, he pulled into a deserted lot and braked to a stop.

Gina frowned and glanced at the snow-laden, empty fields illuminated by his headlights. "Why are we stopping here?"

Leaving the engine idling and the heat on, Zach leaned across the bucket seats and kissed her the way he'd wanted to all day.

Pulling away, he shrugged out of his coat and climbed over the console to join Gina in her seat. She shed her coat, too. They reclined the seat back as far as it would go and made out like teenage kids, touching each other everywhere and breathing hard.

After a while, dangerously close to losing control, he pulled back. "I want to make love with you, Gina, but when I do, it will be in a bed, not here in the truck."

"We could go to the house, but Sophie and Gloria are there. Let's go to your place."

The modest trailer wasn't the custom-built, five-bedroom home Zach had once owned, but there weren't any hotels in Saddlers Prairie, and it was the best option. He nodded. "After the party."

"All right." She leaned up and kissed him, a kiss filled with passion and promise.

Hard and aching, he returned to the driver's seat and headed for the Lucky A.

## Chapter Seventeen

"Your cell phone is ringing," Sophie called out from the kitchen, where she and Gloria impatiently waited for Zach to take them to the party at the Dawson Ranch. Uncle Redd had hitched a ride with his next-door neighbor.

On her way downstairs, Gina frowned and hurried into the living room, where she'd left the phone. She knew at a glance that it was a from the credit-card company, reminding her that she was over her limit and late on a payment.

A payment she couldn't afford to make until her paycheck came in next week. After that check, she had one more coming, plus her vacation pay. What would she do then?

Flooded with shame, she silenced the call and stuffed the phone into her purse.

"Who was that?" Gloria asked.

"Sales call."

"Six days before Christmas? You'd think those people would give it a rest. You look very festive in that red sweater, by the way."

"Thanks." She hadn't brought any Christmassy outfits with her and would have liked to buy herself something new for tonight. But with her money situation, that was out.

"Your hair is pretty, too. I've never seen it swept up that way. Zach will like that." Sophie gave her a knowing look.

In the three days since the trip to Elk Ridge, her family had doubled the sly looks and bold comments without the slightest encouragement from Gina or Zach. She'd barely mentioned Zach's name, and he hadn't stopped by the house.

But she thought constantly of him and what they would do together at his trailer later tonight. She was playing with fire but couldn't make herself stop.

Zach knocked at the door, and she let him in. His appreciative gaze flitted over her sweater and pleated skirt. "I like that outfit."

Her heart rate bumped a few notches. "Thank you." She took in the dark green sweater that lovingly hugged his broad shoulders and the black dress pants that emphasized his flat belly and narrow hips. "I like what you're wearing, too. Green is nice and festive."

His eyes warmed, filled with promise for the night ahead. "Red and green—you two look like a matched set," Gloria quipped. "You can admire each other more later. Let's get to that party."

Zach turned his attention to her cousins. "You both look beautiful. Let's go."

He helped everyone into their coats. When he reached for Gloria's arm, she sniffed. "Now that my hand is better, I've gotten pretty good with these crutches. I can do this myself."

"Yes, ma'am." Zach held up his hands and stepped back, far enough to give her space but close enough to catch her if she slipped. "After you."

Tonight he was driving one of the ranch Jeeps, which was roomier than his truck. Gloria sat up front so that she could stretch out her leg, and Gina and Sophie sat in the back.

Over the past few weeks, Gina had been at the Dawsons' house a few times for evening get-togethers with Jenny, Meg and other friends. She loved everything about the family home, which was generations old and spacious enough for the Dawson brothers and their families, yet warm and comfortable.

Gina hadn't seen the tree, though. Standing in a corner in the great room, it had to be eight feet tall and was bright with lights and ornaments. Men, women and children filled every room on the main floor with conversation and laughter.

Gina helped Gloria sit down and made sure she had food and drink. Then she filled a plate for herself, taking it with her while she greeted friends.

People she hadn't seen since the funeral and hadn't had much of a chance to talk to told her how pleased they were that she was staying through the holidays. Some asked about her work and praised her for doing so well. Feeling like a big fake, she smiled and pretended her life was as cushy and great as everyone believed.

Her conscience ate at her. Sooner or later, she would have to tell them the truth. The thought of losing the respect of Zach, her family and friends bothered her so much that she barely touched the food on her plate.

With the sixth sense that seemed to kick in when Zach was near, she could tell that he was watching her. Standing across the room, he raised his eyebrow. Gina managed a smile. He jerked his head toward a hallway, signaling her to follow him. When they met there, he pulled her through a closed door that turned out to be the powder room.

He shut the door, backed her against it and kissed her. Gina's money troubles melted away. She forgot she was broke, forgot she was in a bathroom at a Christmas party. She forgot everything but Zach.

Still kissing her, he cupped her breast and pushed his thigh between her legs. She moaned into his mouth.

"That's just a sample of what I want to do with you later," he said, nuzzling her ear. "Let's see if we can't get your cousins out of here soon."

IMPATIENT FOR GINA to arrive, Zach checked his watch for what had to be the dozenth time. It had been nearly an hour since he'd dropped her and her cousins off at the house. She'd wanted to wait until her cousins were safely in bed before coming back to Zach's.

Suddenly he heard the old truck rumble to a stop in front of the trailer.

He opened the door and gestured her inside. "Hey."

"Hi." She hesitated a moment, almost as if she feared crossing the threshold.

He tried to see the trailer through her eyes. He'd tidied up and changed the sheets and towels, but no amount of cleaning could change the fact that his place was small and shabby, something he wouldn't have set foot in back in Houston, let alone live in.

Not ideal for a woman used to the finer trappings money bought. Sometimes Zach missed the luxury and comfort he'd once taken for granted, but at least here his conscience was clear.

He helped her out of her coat and hung it on the hook on the door. She'd taken her hair down but was still in her party clothes, a snug sweater, a short, pleated skirt and sexy heels that made her great legs look impossibly long.

He gestured toward the sofa, which was half the size of the one in Lucky's living room and a lot saggier. "I opened a bottle of wine."

"I barely sipped my glass at the party. How did you know?" She sat down. Her skirt rode up, revealing a nice length of creamy thigh. "I didn't think Sophie and Gloria would ever go to bed," she said, sipping from her glass. "I felt like a teenager, waiting for my parents to fall asleep so I could sneak out."

Zach joined her and sampled his own glass. "We should've just told them you were coming over."

"Give them even more ideas about us? No, thanks."

He slipped his arm around her. "I want you to know that I'm clean."

"Me, too." She gulped her wine.

"Nervous?"

"A little. I'm not sure why."

Zach was pretty sure the trailer and his blue-collar job had something to do with it. If he were smart, he'd tell her that this was a bad idea and he'd changed his mind.

He wanted her too much for that. "I know a great way to relax you." After setting both their glasses on the coffee table, he directed her to turn around so that her back faced him.

He began to knead her shoulders. She was small and delicate boned.

"That feels good," she murmured, bowing her head.

Her tense muscles quickly softened until she was leaning into his hands. Brushing her hair aside, Zach kissed the crook of her shoulder and felt her shiver. "Better?"

"I'm putty in your hands."

"Just wait." He tugged her sweater up and massaged her slender back. Her skin was soft and smooth.

Her breathing quickened, growing jagged as he unfastened her bra and cupped her breasts from behind.

With a soft moan, she arched into his hands. Her nipples hardened to sharp points.

How he wanted her. Hungry, his body pulsing, he turned her to face him, pulled her sweater over her head and got rid of his own.

Her breasts were full and taut.

"You are so beautiful."

Tracing her nipples with his finger, he thrilled to her shudder of pleasure. Moving from one nipple to the other, he followed his finger with his tongue until she was restless and panting and he was in danger of losing control.

"I don't want to make love with you on this old couch," he said and pulled her up.

He led her into his bedroom. The double bed took up most of the space. Gina stepped out of her heels and unzipped her skirt. It pooled at her feet, leaving her in thigh highs and bikini panties. "You look hot," he said.

She gave him a smile as if she was well aware of that and started to peel off the stockings.

Zach stopped her. "Leave those on."

"You like them."

"Very much. But the panties can go."

As she stepped out of them, Zach quickly shed his pants and boxers. They were both naked, both studying each other. Her womanly body awed him.

She stepped into his arms. His—for tonight.

She was smooth and soft and warm, and she fit perfectly against him. Kissing her, he backed her to the bed and eased her down. He slid his hand between her legs. She was wet and hot.

Zach groaned, and his body demanded release. Dear God, he wanted to be inside of her.

But not just yet. Kneeling between her thighs, he parted her folds and explored her most sensitive place. A sound that was half moan, half sigh filled the air.

She shifted restlessly, caught hold of his ears and

tugged him closer. Moments later, she climaxed. When she relaxed and went still, he kissed her inner thigh, her stomach. Claimed her mouth.

She reached between them. If she touched him there, he would lose it.

"Easy." Clasping her wrists, he pushed her onto her back. "Are you ready for more?"

"Yes. This time, inside me."

He sheathed himself. In one thrust he entered her.

She was slick and hot and tight, and she felt so damn good. Wanting to take it slow, Zach closed his eyes and for a long, tortured moment didn't move.

But Gina hugged his hips with her thighs and clenched her muscles around him and he forgot all about going slowly. She began to make sweet sounds that signaled her climax was near.

On the brink himself, Zach thrust fast and deep until the world disappeared. Together they exploded in blinding pleasure.

Later, drained and utterly satisfied, he collapsed beside her.

Gina let out a satisfied sigh. Zach kissed the top of her head. She smelled like her flowery shampoo and sex, a heady combination. "I'm glad we finally did that," he said.

"Mmm, me, too." She kissed his ribs and snuggled close.

Soon her breathing eased and he knew she was sleeping.

He cupped her hip. Murmuring, she moved closer. His chest was full, and he knew that what he felt for Gina went way beyond the fantastic sex they'd just shared. But he'd already known that.

As special as she was, she was straight out of his old world, driven by money and success. Like his family and his ex, she wouldn't understand why he'd left that life behind. For sure he wasn't about to open himself to that by explaining about his past.

Any kind of relationship beyond sex was doomed to fail.

Uneasy, he stared at the ceiling and wondered what he was doing. *Relax,* he told himself. *Gina doesn't want a relationship with me, either.* This was about sex—nothing more.

He drifted off to sleep.

WITHOUT INTENDING TO, Gina had fallen asleep in Zach's bed. Before she even opened her eyes, she could tell that he had drifted off, too. The room was dark, but light from the other room spilled in and she could easily make out the fake wood walls, decor from an era long past. The watch Uncle Lucky had left him ticked softly on the knotty-pine dresser. There wasn't room for any other furniture.

Zach's entire trailer was smaller than Uncle Lucky's kitchen and living room combined—barely big enough to accommodate one person.

How could he stand living here?

In his sleep, he cupped her bottom possessively in his big hands. Fresh desire flooded her. Never mind where he lived—she wanted him to touch her like this forever.

But she wanted more than that—a lot more. She wanted Zach to have a good job and a future, wanted to know about his past. She wanted the security of her job at Andersen, Coats and Mueller and her year-end bonus.

Unfortunately, what she wanted was the opposite of what she had. If only...

Beside her, Zach stirred. He was awake and aroused. His fingers slid between her legs, spreading heat through her and erasing her thoughts. He kissed her passionately, and she forgot about everything but the here and now.

Some time later, she smiled up at him. "That was even better than the first time."

"The best way in the world to wake up. Makes you wonder why we wasted so much time getting here. We should have done this weeks ago."

"I'm not wired that way." She traced the planes of his face. His cheekbones and regal nose, his strong chin and jaw. His eyelashes were longer than any man had a right to.

Such a handsome face. With an inward sigh, she admitted to herself that want to or not, she was completely in love with him.

He opened his eyes and stared into her soul with a tenderness she hadn't seen before. He cared for her, but he didn't really know her.

Didn't know that instead of a being the successful marketing executive he thought she was, she'd lost her job and everything she'd worked for. Worse, she was in a huge financial bind.

She was a complete fraud.

*Tell him,* her conscience whispered. The very thought terrified her. And have him change his mind about her, look at her with the same disgust she held for herself? She couldn't bear that.

"You okay?" he asked.

No, and it was best to change the subject. "I was thinking about how little I really know about your past."

His expression shuttered. "You said you wouldn't ask again."

He didn't trust her, and her heart recoiled. She grabbed gratefully onto the feeling. Better to feel hurt than guilty. "I changed my mind. What are you hiding from me?"

Stony faced, he sat up. "It's late."

Gina sat up, too, pulling the covers with her. "So you can do the most intimate physical things with me, but you can't share your personal stuff." Add utter hypocrite to her list of flaws.

"What we just shared was pretty damn personal. I care about you, Gina, but this is as personal as you're going to get from me." He rose from the bed and put on his boxers.

"I'll leave as soon as I'm dressed." Holding the blanket around her like a protective shield, she retrieved her clothes. "Where's the bathroom?"

"Down the hall, to your left."

"Go back to sleep," she said. "I'll let myself out."

Zach didn't argue.

Fifteen minutes later, feeling more alone than she could ever remember, she tiptoed into the house and made her way up the stairs.

## Chapter Eighteen

In need of a friendly ear, Gina called Autumn the following day and invited her to lunch. "Let's meet at the Pizza Palace," she said.

"Love to. Hold on while I see if one of the boys can watch April." Seconds later, she was back. "It'll have to be a quick lunch. I can meet you at twelve, but I have to be back by one."

Shortly before noon, Gina found an empty booth and sat down to wait for her friend.

It wasn't long before Autumn slid in across from her, her cheeks flushed from the cold. "What a great party last night."

"It was."

A teenage girl took their orders. When she left, Autumn smiled. "You and Zach are seeing each other while you're in town, huh?"

"I'm not sure." Gina bit her lip. "That's one of the reasons I called you. I really need to talk to someone."

"What's the matter?"

"It's pretty embarrassing. You won't tell anyone, right?"

"Not even Cody."

Satisfied, Gina lowered her voice. "Zach and I made love last night."

"The way you were looking at each other at the party, I'm not surprised." Autumn frowned. "You don't seem happy about that. Was the sex bad?"

Still glowing from their lovemaking, Gina shook her head. "It was wonderful. But Zach doesn't trust me. He's told me a little about his family, but he won't talk about his past—where he worked, what he did there and why he left Houston. I can't help but wonder what he's hiding."

Autumn nodded but didn't comment. She listened without judgment, which was exactly what Gina needed.

Gina wasn't going to share her own secrets, but once she started talking, her troubles spilled out and she unloaded everything—her strong feelings for Zach and why they scared her, her job situation and her money troubles.

"Here I am, questioning Zach for not telling me about his past, when my own life is a total sham," she finished. "Pretty pathetic, isn't it?"

Autumn shrugged. She didn't seem nearly as disappointed in her as Gina had imagined. "Stuff happens."

The waitress delivered their food. As soon as she moved away from the table, Autumn went on. "The job thing isn't your fault."

"No, but my financial situation is."

"You can fix that. Trust me, I know—I was in the same boat when I went to work as Cody's housekeeper. You'll get another job and everything will be fine." Autumn dug into her lunch.

Having eaten little since long before the Dawson's party, Gina was famished. For a few minutes she and Autumn both concentrated on eating.

"I'm not sure what to do about Zach," she said when she finally came up for air. "Should I trust him?"

"You're the only one who can answer that. What does your heart tell you?"

"I'm in love with him, and I think he cares about me, too."

Autumn nodded thoughtfully. "Maybe if you trust Zach enough to share your problems with him, he'll open up to you."

Gina had never considered that.

"It all boils down to what you want," Autumn said as they finished the meal. "What do you want, Gina?"

She'd been mulling that over since Kevin had suggested she think about it. "I'm not sure," she admitted.

"You'll figure it out. I hate to cut our conversation short, but I have to get back."

They paid and walked out to their cars.

Before they parted ways, Gina hugged her friend. "Thanks for listening."

"Anytime. Let me know what happens, okay? And merry Christmas."

On the drive back to the Lucky A, Gina thought hard about what she wanted.

Only weeks ago, her dream had been to make vice president at Andersen, Coats and Mueller and go on climbing the ranks from there. The commonsense part of her wanted a good job in marketing and the potential to advance. But her heart wanted Zach, and fighting with her heart was a losing battle.

Autumn was right—if she wanted a relationship with him, she needed to be honest. The very thought terrified her. He might not be as easygoing about her situation as Autumn had been. Gina would have to tell her family, too.

She swallowed. Could she risk the humiliation of admitting she'd been living a lie?

She wasn't sure she was brave enough.

FALLING FOR GINA was about the stupidest thing Zach had ever done, and over the next few days, he called himself ten kinds of fool. He steered clear of her. She didn't try to find him, either.

His one consolation was that they seemed to be of the same mind. Neither of them wanted a relationship. That was a relief—or so he told himself.

On Christmas Eve day he was in a foul mood. Hard work always helped take his mind off his problems, but he'd worked over Thanksgiving. For the next two days, Pete, Bert and Chet were responsible for doing all the chores.

Early that afternoon, Redd phoned him. "Merry Christmas. The dogs and I just arrived at the house. We're spending the night. The usual friends and neighbors will be stopping by later this afternoon, and we want you here."

Zach was in no mood to spend the holiday with the Arnetts, particularly Gina. He doubted she wanted to see him, either. But her family expected him there. "What time?" he asked.

They settled on three o'clock—an hour away.

Zach was wandering around the small trailer, waiting for the time to pass, when someone knocked on his door.

Grateful for the distraction, he opened it. To his surprise, Gina stood on the stoop.

He drank in the sight of her. "Redd called a little while ago. I said I'd come at three. What are you doing here?"

"Merry Christmas." She fiddled with her glove and tried to smile. "May I come in?"

Wondering what she wanted, he shrugged. "Sure."

He moved back so that she could step inside.

ZACH LOOKED WARY and tired, as if he hadn't been sleeping. Gina wasn't sleeping well, either. There was too much to think about, too much at stake. Weighing the risks of honesty versus continuing to live a lie had consumed her, and she couldn't sleep or eat, let alone enjoy the Christmas festivities.

She was so miserable that Gloria and Sophie had stopped bickering, uniting to shower her with pitying looks. Even Sugar and Bit avoided her, slinking past with their tails between their legs.

Her conscience was eating her alive. If she didn't do something soon, she would make herself sick.

It was time to tell the truth.

Zach took her coat and hung it on the hook. "You want coffee?"

At the moment, she couldn't put anything in her stomach to save her life. "No, but I would like to sit down."

He gestured toward the little table in his miniscule kitchen. They sat, their knees almost touching.

"If this is about the other night..." He cleared his throat. "I shouldn't have let you leave like that."

"We both said things." She wasn't sure exactly how to begin, so she spoke from the heart. "I know you care about me, Zach, and I have feelings for you, too. Strong feelings. But I need to tell you something, and... Well, I'm pretty sure that once I do, your opinion of me will change."

Any wariness vanished under a quizzical look.

"When Gloria broke her ankle and I called my boss, he was pretty unhappy that I wanted to stay here," she said. "In a nutshell, he gave me a choice—either leave the company or come back as an assistant." The idea was so repugnant that she shuddered. "I can't do that. He's not going to give me my year-end bonus, either, and you have no idea how badly I need it."

Afraid of what she'd see in Zach's eyes, she looked down at her hands. "I'm in real trouble. I can't pay my bills, and collectors are starting to call. I have one more paycheck and my vacation pay coming. After that..." She swallowed around a lump of fear. "I may have to declare bankruptcy. I didn't think I was anything like my parents, but I guess I'm like my dad. He spent money he didn't have to impress people, and I did that, too."

There. It was out.

Her cheeks burning with humiliation, she forced herself to meet Zach's gaze. To her surprise, she saw only warmth.

"Back up to the part about your feelings for me," he said. "I'm a lowly ranch foreman."

"I know, and go figure. I've been thinking about your past. I don't understand why you're hiding it from me, but the truth is, I already know everything I need to about you. You're a good man with a big heart—that's what matters."

The last part was the hardest to say, and she cleared her throat. "Now you know that I lied about my life. If you don't... If you're not interested in me anymore, I understand."

"Because your jackass boss fired you and you have money problems?" Zach shook his head. "Those things don't matter to me. I'm still crazy about you."

Gina couldn't quite believe her ears. "Even if I have to sell the ranch to pay down my bills?"

Across the table, he caught hold of her hands. "That'd be a real bummer, but even then."

She was so overcome that her eyes filled. "Zach Horton, I love you."

"Yeah?" A smile started at his lips and spread until his eyes lit up and crinkled at the corners. "I love you, too. Come here, and I'll show you just how much."

Zach pulled her close and kissed her, and nothing else mattered.

Later, when she was lying naked and sated in his bed,

her cell phone rang. "I better get that." She pulled out of his arms and glanced at the screen. "It's Gloria. I told her I was going out, and I'm sure she wonders where I am."

"Tell her you're with me."

"I will."

When she hung up, she reached for her clothes. "It's time to go to the house."

"We still have a lot to talk about," Zach said.

"We'll have to save that conversation for another time. Please don't say anything to my family about my job or finances. I'm not ready to tell them."

"I won't say a word."

## *Chapter Nineteen*

Later that evening, after the guests had consumed the Christmas Eve meal and headed home, and Gloria, Redd, Sophie and the dogs were safely asleep, Zach sat on the sofa with his arm around Gina. Only the fire and the Christmas-tree lights lit the room.

"What a beautiful tree," she said, snuggling close.

"You're beautiful." He kissed her, her soft sigh wrapping around his heart.

Gina loved him. He felt good about that and awed that she'd been honest with him. It hadn't been easy for her to tell him about losing her job or her money worries, but she'd told him all the same.

Her courage inspired him, and before he left the house tonight, he intended to bare his soul to her. She deserved to know the kind of man he used to be. Like his family, she might not understand why he'd chosen to give up his old life, might think he was crazy. She could decide she didn't want him, after all. Dread knotted his gut.

"Zach? You're frowning."

"Am I?" Not quite ready to tell her, he forced a light expression. "I think your family's onto us."

"You mean because they made sure we sat next to each other at dinner and turned in early so that we could be alone?" Gina rolled her eyes. "I should never have told them we were together when they called this afternoon."

"Are you going to tell them about your job?"

"Yes, tomorrow. I'm not looking forward to that."

"They're still going to love you," he said.

He only hoped that Gina would still love him when he shared his past.

"They're going to be shocked. They're so proud of me, and I hate letting them down."

"They'll get over it."

"Will they?" She tried to smile. "I feel lost, Zach, and I will until I find a new job. Plus, they think I have all this money. I need to tell them, but I wish I didn't."

"Hey." He smoothed her hair back and smiled into her worried eyes. "You're one of the bravest, strongest people I know, and you can do this."

"Brave and strong. I've never thought of myself as either. Thank you for that." She leaned up and kissed him, a gentle press of the lips not meant to incite passion.

Yet the hunger between them simmered in the air.

Gina checked her watch. "It's getting late and we both need to get some sleep. I wish you could stay here tonight, but with my family in the house…"

"Yeah, that'd feel weird."

Zach needed to go soon, but first it was time to come clean. "Before I leave, there are some things you need to know about me." He let go of her, leaned forward and stared at his hands. "I don't like to talk about my past, but it's time I explained."

Gina sucked in a breath and went still.

"I used to own my own company. Horton Real Estate was a commercial real-estate corporation. I worked long hours and lived for deals and profits, and my company thrived and grew. I met my fiancée when she came to work for me. We lived in a big, custom-built home and owned three cars. Money, love, success—I had it all and should've been happy. But I wasn't. I thought the answer was to cut bigger and better deals.

"A man named Sam Swain owned a choice section of land I coveted. I dreamed of developing it into a premiere shopping mall. Swain wanted to leave it undeveloped and deed his acreage to a land trust."

This next part was hard, and Zach paused and studied the calluses on his palm. Gina reached for his hand, silently offering support. Unable to look at her just yet, he laced his fingers with hers and went on. "I wouldn't let it go. I wined and dined his family, his accountant and his lawyer. I wouldn't let up. Soon everyone Sam trusted, especially his wife and kids, was pressuring him nonstop to take the money and sell. He finally signed off on the deal, but it broke his heart. Literally. Not long after I took possession of the property and broke ground, he dropped dead of a heart attack."

Emotion clogged his throat and he swallowed. "Sam Swain is in his grave because I put him there."

Gina opened her mouth, but he signaled that he wasn't finished. "His death changed me. I no longer wanted to run the business or cut deals. I sold the company and donated some of the proceeds to the land trust Sam favored. My family ridiculed me for that. They still think I'm crazy. Losing their support was rough, but at least my fiancée stood by me."

He gave a humorless laugh. "Or that's what I thought at first. I was mistaken. She broke off the engagement and decided to stay on at the company. A year later she married the man who bought it from me.

"That was around the time I left Houston. I wasn't sure where I wanted to go or what I wanted to do. After drifting for months, I ended up in Saddlers Prairie. I didn't know anything about cattle, but Lucky took a chance on me. He taught me about ranching and showed me how to find joy in simple things like a hard day's work. He advised me to learn from my mistakes and move on." He managed a smile. "I'm still working on that one."

Finished, he bowed his head.

Gina pulled her hand from his, cupped his face and turned his head toward her. "Sam Swain's death wasn't your fault, Zach."

They were the same words his family had repeated countless times, only hers held no scorn. In Gina's eyes he saw only love.

"You're a good man, Zach Horton. That's why I fell in love with you." She smiled. "Even though I fought it tooth and nail."

Zach's heart swelled in his chest. "That's one battle I'm glad you lost."

He kissed her without holding anything back. A long time later, he reluctantly broke away. "I should go." He took her hand and pulled her to her feet.

She loved him, but he wasn't sure love was enough. If she accepted him as he was, he would give her a Christmas gift she would never forget. If not... Well, that just might kill him.

At the back door, he turned to her. "We have..." So much was riding on her and what she wanted, and his voice shook. Zach stopped and cleared his throat. "We have a lot to talk about. I know you want a high-flying corporate executive, but I can't be that man ever again. If you want a future with me, you have to be okay with that."

He left her standing in the door.

THERE WAS SO much to think about, and Gina couldn't sleep. Zach loved her and she loved him.

But was love enough?

She no longer had a big salary to keep her afloat, and neither did he. She didn't want to make the same mistakes her parents had made—she didn't want a marriage plagued with money worries.

Zach had suffered dearly for Sam Swain's death, which hadn't been his fault. His guilt over that made Gina love him all the more. Everything made sense now. His comments about the rat race and his seeming disinterest in the corporate world.

Living a hectic, competitive life hadn't made him happy. It didn't make her happy, either. Nor had her big salary, expensive clothes and nice condo.

If she set aside her money problems, she wouldn't miss her job at all.

That was such a revelation that Gina could no longer lie in bed. She rose and slipped on her robe. Uncle Lucky had taught Zach to find joy in the little things. Why couldn't she do the same? Peering out the window, into the darkness, she noted how the snow caught the moonlight, making the moon twice as bright. The fields sparkled with light.

Such a beautiful ranch and a perfect Christmas Eve night. She could almost imagine Santa and his sleigh flying through the sky.

She smiled with joy. So this was what finding pleasure in little things felt like.

Still grinning, she crept back downstairs. The fire was low but she heard the sizzle of the dying embers. The sound delighted her, and plugging in the Christmas-tree lights only increased her happiness.

She plunked down onto the sofa and, for a while, she simply enjoyed the sights and sounds. Then she thought about other things that made her happy. Not what, *who*.

Zach.

He'd made her laugh countless times and always brightened her day—even when she was mad at him.

Regardless of what he did for a living, life with him would always be blessed with love and joy.

And just like that, Gina let go of her need to be with a man driven to succeed. She let go of her own need to climb the corporate ladder.

It was an odd feeling, trusting that she was good enough to have love and friendship no matter what she did for a living. She would need time to get used to that.

Her debt was an awful burden, and the thought of declaring bankruptcy made her sick to her stomach. She didn't want to do that and needed a new job—soon.

Sometime before dawn, she stumbled upon the solution to her problems. She could hardly wait to share it with Zach and her family.

She tiptoed into the office, wrote a note and wrapped it in Christmas paper. After adding a ribbon and printing Zach's name on the gift card, she slipped it under the tree beneath the other presents.

Humming and feeling strangely energized, she danced up the stairs to shower and dress. Downstairs again, she made the coffee and started the Christmas breakfast casserole.

It was baking in the oven when her family entered the kitchen. Minutes later, Zach showed up.

"Merry Christmas, Zach. I thought about what you said last night, and I'm fine with you—just as you are."

Zach's eyes looked suspiciously bright. Gina's eyes

filled, too. Without the least bit of embarrassment or nervousness, she pulled him down for a kiss.

When they broke apart, the expressions on her family's faces were priceless.

After breakfast, Uncle Redd pushed his chair back. "Let's take our coffee into the living room and open our presents."

It was time to tell her family the truth.

"If you'd all wait a minute." Gina stood and gestured for her family to remain at the table. "There's something I need to tell you."

Wanting Zach's support, she glanced at him. Without hesitation he joined her, grabbing hold of her hand.

Gloria and Sophie gave her knowing looks, and Uncle Redd beamed. They obviously thought that this was a romantic announcement of some kind. They were in for a disappointment.

"This isn't easy for me to say," she said, "and my timing sucks."

They looked concerned now. Zach gave her hand an encouraging squeeze and her story spilled out.

"You don't know this, but a couple of weeks ago my boss fired me," she said, strangely eager to get the words out. "But that's not all. I'm in debt and teetering on bankruptcy. I know how embarrassing that is for you. I'm so ashamed and so sorry to ruin your Christmas this way."

For once, Gloria was speechless.

Sophie clutched her chest. "Oh, cookie, that's terrible."

"We'll be all right, honey," Uncle Redd said. "But what will you do?"

"I'll answer your questions after we open our gifts."

"Now?" Gloria frowned. "This is serious. Don't you want to talk about it?"

Sophie glared at her. "She just said she will later. It's

Christmas, and she doesn't want to think about her problems right now."

"Well, I do."

The sisters glared at each other.

"Girls, please." Uncle Redd shook his head. "Like Sophie says, it's Christmas. Can't you knock it off for a while? If Gina wants to open presents now, so do I."

Her family all looked fondly at her.

Nothing had changed. They felt for her, but they still loved her, just as Zach had said.

She could hardly wait for them to open their gifts.

They headed into the living room, Zach holding her hand until she pushed him into a chair and handed out the presents.

Her family loved the things she'd picked up at the mall. Sophie loved her new earrings and Gloria wrapped herself in her new sweater. Uncle Redd was pleased with his kidskin gloves and Sugar and Bit seemed delighted with their new chew toys.

Gina opened the gift they'd all chipped in to buy her. "Red cowboy boots. I love them! Thank you all."

They gave Zach a display case for his watch.

"What a lovely Christmas," Sophie said.

"Wait—there's something else under the tree." Gloria pointed to the last gift. "It's a skinny little thing. What is it?"

"That's for you, Zach—from me." Gina retrieved the gift from under the tree and handed it to him.

He unwrapped the paper and read the note she'd written. He looked incredulous. "You're not selling the ranch."

"That's right." She smiled. "That's my real present to you all. I'm not sure yet how I'll keep it going, but, Zach,

I hope you'll stay and help me. As soon as I get back to Chicago, I'm going to cut up my credit cards and trade in my Lexus for a practical car I can afford. I'm going to sell my condo, too. I'll use some of the proceeds to pay down my bills and the rest to pay your salary. Will you stay?"

"Where will you be?" he asked.

"I'm going to drive right back here and move into this house. I've decided to start my own marketing/PR business. I'm good at what I do, and I know I can make it work."

Gloria wiped away a tear, Redd cleared his throat and Sophie bawled like a baby.

"I think they like the idea," Zach said. "I sure do."

"So you'll stay on?" Gina asked.

"That depends on what you think of my Christmas gift to you." He pulled an envelope from his pocket and handed it to her.

As GINA READ Zach's card, her jaw dropped, just as he'd imagined it would. He grinned.

"Do you mind if I share this with my family?" she asked. He shook his head. "Zach has offered to buy half the ranch so that we're equal partners." A puzzled frown filled her face. "How can you afford that?"

"I have some money in the bank, money I haven't touched in a long time." He hadn't known what to do with the proceeds from the sale of his company. Now he did. "I figure that with your marketing smarts and my business know-how, we'll get the dude ranch up and running in no time." He grasped hold of Gina's hands. "If things work out the way I hope, we'll be much more than business partners."

He wanted to go on, but emotion clogged his throat. He had to swallow and clear it several times. "What do you say?"

Gina's eyes filled with warmth and love. "I feel like I'm in a fairy tale. Yes, Zach, I'll be your partner in every way. Merry Christmas, everyone."

\* \* \* \* \*

# REQUEST YOUR FREE BOOKS!
## 2 FREE NOVELS PLUS 2 FREE GIFTS!

### HARLEQUIN

## *American ★ Romance*
### LOVE, HOME & HAPPINESS

**YES!** Please send me 2 FREE Harlequin® American Romance® novels and my 2 FREE gifts (gifts are worth about $10). After receiving them, if I don't wish to receive any more books, I can return the shipping statement marked "cancel." If I don't cancel, I will receive 4 brand-new novels every month and be billed just $4.74 per book in the U.S. or $5.24 per book in Canada. That's a savings of at least 14% off the cover price! It's quite a bargain! Shipping and handling is just 50¢ per book in the U.S. and 75¢ per book in Canada.* I understand that accepting the 2 free books and gifts places me under no obligation to buy anything. I can always return a shipment and cancel at any time. Even if I never buy another book, the two free books and gifts are mine to keep forever.

154/354 HDN F4YN

Name _____
(PLEASE PRINT)

Address _____ Apt. # _____

City _____ State/Prov. _____ Zip/Postal Code _____

Signature (if under 18, a parent or guardian must sign)

### Mail to the **Harlequin® Reader Service:**
**IN U.S.A.:** P.O. Box 1867, Buffalo, NY 14240-1867
**IN CANADA:** P.O. Box 609, Fort Erie, Ontario L2A 5X3

**Want to try two free books from another line?**
**Call 1-800-873-8635 or visit www.ReaderService.com.**

* Terms and prices subject to change without notice. Prices do not include applicable taxes. Sales tax applicable in N.Y. Canadian residents will be charged applicable taxes. Offer not valid in Quebec. This offer is limited to one order per household. Not valid for current subscribers to Harlequin American Romance books. All orders subject to credit approval. Credit or debit balances in a customer's account(s) may be offset by any other outstanding balance owed by or to the customer. Please allow 4 to 6 weeks for delivery. Offer available while quantities last.

**Your Privacy**—The Harlequin® Reader Service is committed to protecting your privacy. Our Privacy Policy is available online at www.ReaderService.com or upon request from the Harlequin Reader Service.

We make a portion of our mailing list available to reputable third parties that offer products we believe may interest you. If you prefer that we not exchange your name with third parties, or if you wish to clarify or modify your communication preferences, please visit us at www.ReaderService.com/consumerschoice or write to us at Harlequin Reader Service Preference Service, P.O. Box 9062, Buffalo, NY 14269. Include your complete name and address.

HAR13R

SPECIAL EXCERPT FROM

HARLEQUIN®

## American Romance®

*Read on for a sneak peek at*
*HIS CHRISTMAS SWEETHEART*
*by* New York Times *bestselling author*
*Cathy McDavid*

*The handsome ranch hand Will Desarro is a man of few*
*words, but Miranda Staley soon discovers that beneath*
*that quiet exterior beats a heart of gold.*

Miranda grinned. Will Dessaro was absolutely adorable when flustered—and he was flustered a lot around her.

How had she coexisted in the same town with him for all these years and not noticed him?

Then came the day of the fire and the order to evacuate within two hours. He'd shown up on her doorstep, strong, silent, capable, and provided the help she'd needed to rally and load her five frightened and uncooperative residents into the van.

She couldn't have done it without him. And he'd been visiting Mrs. Litey regularly ever since.

Thank the Lord her house had been spared. The same couldn't be said for several hundred other homes and buildings in Sweetheart, including many on her own street. Her beautiful and quaint hometown had been brought to its knees in a matter of hours and still hadn't recovered five months later.

"I hate to impose…." Miranda glanced over her shoulder, making sure Will had accompanied her into the kitchen. "There's a leak in the pipe under the sink. The repairman can't fit me in his schedule till Monday, and the leak's worsening by the hour." She paused. "You're good with tools, aren't you?"

"Good enough." He blushed.

Sweet heaven, he was a cutie.

Wavy brown hair that insisted on falling rakishly over one brow. Dark eyes. Cleft in his chin. Breathtakingly tall. He towered above her five-foot-three frame.

If only he'd respond to one of the many dozen hints she'd dropped and ask her on a date.

"Do you mind taking a peek for me?" She gestured toward the open cabinet doors beneath the sink. "I'd really appreciate it."

"Sure." His gaze went to the toolbox on the floor. "You have an old towel or pillow I can use?"

That had to be the longest sentence he'd ever uttered in her presence.

"Be right back." She returned shortly with an old beach towel folded in a large square.

By then, Will had set his cowboy hat on the table and rolled up his sleeves.

Nice arms, she noted. Tanned, lightly dusted with hair and corded with muscles.

She flashed him another brilliant smile and handed him the towel.

His blush deepened.

Excellent. Message sent and received.

*Will Miranda lasso her shy cowboy this holiday season?*
*Find out in*
HIS CHRISTMAS SWEETHEART
*by* New York Times *bestselling author Cathy McDavid*
*Available November 5, 2013,*
*only from Harlequin® American Romance®.*

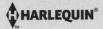

# American Romance®

## To Love, Honor…and Multiply!

Becoming a husband and family man in the middle of a
raging land feud wasn't the destiny Galen Callahan saw for
himself. But once he laid eyes on Rose Carstairs, he knew
the bouncy blonde with the warrior heart was his future.
Now, with Rancho Diablo under siege, the eldest Callahan
sibling will do whatever it takes to protect his new wife
and triplets. With Callahan lives and legacy on the line,
Galen has a new mission: to vanquish a dangerous enemy
and bring his family together in time for Christmas!

### A *Callahan Christmas Miracle*
by *USA TODAY* bestselling author
# TINA LEONARD

Available November 5,
from Harlequin® American Romance®.

**HARLEQUIN**®

# American Romance®

## A Small Town Thanksgiving
### by MARIE FERRARELLA

Ghostwriter Samantha Monroe has just arrived
in Forever, Texas, to turn a remarkable woman's
two-hundred-year-old journals into a personal memoir.
The Rodriguez clan welcomes her with open arms…
and awakens Sam's fierce yearning to be part of a family.
But it's the eldest son, intensely private rancher
Mike Rodriguez, who awakens her passion.

Delving into the past has made Sam hungry for a
future—with Mike. The next move is up to him—if he
doesn't make it, the best woman to ever happen to him
just might waltz back out of his life forever!

**Available November 5,
from Harlequin® American Romance®.**

HAR75479

# American Romance®

## Christmas Miracles Do Happen!

Cabe Jensen hates Christmas. After losing his beloved wife, the holidays are nothing but a painful reminder of all that was good in his world. When his best friend asks to get married at his ranch, Cabe has no idea that it's to be a Christmas wedding! The worst part is he has to work with Saedra Robbins—a friend of the groom—on the plans.

Trouble is, she's making him feel things he'd rather forget. All Cabe knows is he can't stop thinking about kissing her….

# *A Cowboy's Christmas Wedding*
## by PAMELA BRITTON

**Available November 5,
from Harlequin® American Romance®.**

# Love the Harlequin book you just read?

Your opinion matters.

Review this book on your favorite book site, review site, blog or your own social media properties and share your opinion with other readers!

**Be sure to connect with us at:**
Harlequin.com/Newsletters
Facebook.com/HarlequinBooks
Twitter.com/HarlequinBooks